Angels Touch

C. S. Clifford

First published in Great Britain 2022

ISBN: 9 781739 080112

Printed and bound in the UK

A catalogue record of this book is available from the British Library

Edited by Clive Clarke

Cover by Laura Wilde

www.csclifford.co.uk

Books for Older Readers
By C. S. Clifford

THE NAVAJO SERIES

Part 1. ACCEPTANCE	ISBN: 9 780993 195754
Part 2. QUEST	ISBN: 9 780993 195761
Part 3. DETOUR	ISBN: 9 780993 195785
Part 4. PENNANCE	ISBN: 9 781999 361143

THE THIRD MILLENIUM SERIES

ICE AGE	ISBN: 9 781999 361174

THE CHAMELEON SERIES

CHAMELEON ORIGIN	ISBN: 9 781999 361167
CHAMELEON DAWN	ISBN: 9 781739 080150

THE ALONE SERIES

ALONE	ISBN: 9 781739 080136
STILL ALONE	ISBN: 9 781739 080143

THE OUTCAST SERIES

EXCLUSION ZONE	ISBN: 9 781739 080129

STAND ALONE BOOKS

DO YOU SEE ME?	ISBN: 9 781739 080105
ANGELS TOUCH	ISBN: 9 781739 080112

Unselfish sacrifices offer
rewards unimagined.

For those who love a good
story, and for all those I taught
over the years.

To Savanah

Best Wishes

Chapter 1:

The sea was tortured. Waves pounded shingle, shooting plumes of spray upward, instantly flogged by a turbulent wind and eventually falling a distance away. White horses elevated the sea from an otherwise dead slate-grey colour; their random dance heaving, a partnership of conflicting tide and wind.

There was no respite from the macabre scene as, raising his head, he witnessed low-slung, filthy-coloured cumulus clouds, flying at incredible speeds across a hidden sky. Rain was imminent, heavy rain. A dawn sun had threatened to materialise but had lost the battle with the shrouding duvet stretching from horizon to horizon.

Nothing here lifted the spirit which, months ago, had shone so brightly, before gradually eroding, coffee beans in a grinder. What hope was there? What more could he do? How else could he promote himself in the modern world? His sole mission, to gain opportunity to join those really living, those with purpose and direction, and who radiated a smile of warmth in the comfort of their achievements.

The weather's mood reflected his demeanour. Shoulders slumped, head hung low, a sad, defeated look on an otherwise serene and gentle face. No feature marked him for additional attention except for unusually dark-green eyes, currently veiled by weighted eyelids.

Michael had sat for two hours, staring into oblivion, an unconscious dare to the Rain God to dump his load on him. He no longer cared, nothing mattered? Maybe the rain would wash his troubles away, better still, cleanse the diet of negativity presenting itself every time he sought employment. The countless times he heard, *there's nothing right now, you're not the right candidate for the job, or reapply after gaining experience.*

The single task his father had requested, upon completion of school, was simple, as far as he was concerned. *Go to university or get a job, your choice.* He'd repeated it numerous times since, too many times! Did he believe Michael hadn't tried? Hell, he only had to examine his finger tips to see the wear from completing application after application on his laptop. He no longer discerned between jobs he was suited, and unsuited for, he applied for all, every single one he found, without hope, mostly from a sense of duty towards his father and in reality, there were no other options.

All his friends had jobs, all earning, contributing to society, as his father referred to it. Most worked unsocial hours for minimum wages in a variety of fast-food restaurants. Several achieved work in the building industry, or worked for their fathers. Impossible for him, his father worked for the man. This was not what they led him to expect after leaving school. Get qualifications, get a meaningful job with a future. Yeah, right! What a joke, a joke or a pack of lies. All they cared about was making sure the school hit its quota of GCSE passes and finishing high in the rankings.

The first drop of rain hit his face above an eye. It startled him, for a moment transporting him from the thoughts that repeatedly nagged daily, eroding the essence of his worth. A second connected with his cheek. *Go on, why not, wash me away? I'm a waste of time, no good to anyone,* he mused, as another drop hit his chin.

Then it came. Large heavy drops effortlessly permeating his layers of clothing, ink to the blotting paper. He felt the chill sting, soaked before he could stand. His legs, dead from sitting too long without movement, caused him to curse, as did the realisation of knowing his sorry state would not impress the man at the Employment Office, organised to help him find employment.

If anyone saw him then, they would believe he had lost all semblance of common sense. Standing in the middle of nowhere on a shingle beach, he bent, trying to massage life into his dead thighs. They blatantly refused to work, while the rain bounced off waterlogged clothing and beat him in a random rhythm.

Had he been the person he was a year ago, with hopes and expectations, he would be laughing at himself and probably impersonating Gene Kelly's singing in the rain, one of his mother's favourite films. But that was a year ago. A different and beaten Michael walked painfully back towards the road, with a sunken face, hollow eyes and without a shred of hope in his heart.

Reaching it, he followed it towards town, a mile away; no sign of the rain easing. The public conveniences in George Street had one of those incredibly powerful hand driers. He could remove and wring out his shirt and semi-dry it; he couldn't do the same for his jeans; let's be honest, if anybody else walked in… But then, why would anybody venture out in this, if avoidable?

The chill permeated deeper, he could murder a cup of tea, preferably one like his aunt used to make. She did it the old-fashioned way, real tea-leaves in a pot and poured, too hot to drink, into porcelain cups. The splash of milk offered was an exaggeration, but two spoons of sugar neutered the strength of the brew and nobody made a better cup of tea.

The local Wimpy made an excellent pot of tea, and control of milk and sugar content was independent. He checked the loose change in his pocket. He had enough, a plan was hatched. The drier first, the Wimpy second, and at least an hour to warm, if not completely dry, before his appointment. A meeting with a stranger who didn't know him or his capabilities. Would there be another barrage of promises destined to remain unfulfilled, or would somebody finally help him secure work.

Chapter 2:

An hour later he left the fast-food restaurant and head to a building everybody detested, unless you were claiming income support, unemployment benefit or whatever they called it now.

For Michael not optional. In his family, nobody claimed from the state, it wasn't done. You stayed penniless until you found work. His father explained it kept you focussed on actually finding work. *Handouts make you lethargic, lazy; it changed people, not for the better.* To a point Michael accepted his wisdom, he knew families who had third generation benefit collectors, but he needed money for busses or trains, not all jobs were local, and people were expected to travel no matter how poorly paid their jobs.

Standing outside the building did nothing to boost his spirits. It was grey, stone, about as cold as any building could appear. What was it about today? Everything seemed grey, morbid and dead, mirroring his opinions of himself. Wasn't it bad enough he felt this way without seeing mirrored reflections of his mood everywhere? Even the windows rising regimentally in columns, were layered with grey filth on every level; probably started accumulating in the sixties when the building was built.

The reasons for visiting here were many. Some came to pay their council tax, or rent; some sought benefits of various types. But there was more. A multitude of offices above the ground floor existed, and he had no knowledge what service or help was offered there.

An office on the fifth floor was his target, used by a man called Brian Maxwell, a specialist in helping people get employment. Independent from government or council, he was trying to make a difference to local young adults, so the claim in the local paper advert suggested.

Michael walked towards the lift; his mind still focussed on the problems he faced daily. He missed the notice warning the lift was temporarily out of order, almost tripping on the stand holding it. He scanned for the stairs, spotting them by the entrance. Typical! He made the return journey and climbed. Each landing offered a new floor and a solid door preventing a glimpse inside. The surroundings mirrored his earlier mood, concrete stairs, whitewashed walls, in need of painting, and grey doors. Each landing identical to the previous; stairs sweeping around before ascending; the promise of something different on the next floor, never materialising.

Reaching the fifth, he slowed his breathing from the climb. Glancing at his damp shirt, he tried to stretch out the creases, formed when he wrung it out. He was a mess, knew it, and felt it. He stared at the door, wondering what lay beyond it. Could Brian help him find employment and was there a hidden cost for the service? As an independent, it couldn't be free, surely. Reaching out, he grasped the handle, pushed down and stepped through into a large open space.

A receptionist sat at a desk a few feet in front and he walked towards her.

"Hello. I'm Michael Ferguson, I've an appointment with Brian Maxwell at twelve-thirty."

The woman glanced up, staring impassively.

"Door six, take a seat, you'll be called when ready." The voice cold and hard, uncaring, uninterested.

"Thanks."

There were doors everywhere, all numbered, nine in total leading to individual offices. Each faced the centre of the space from a slightly different direction, except the one he'd passed through. Apart from numbers, no other details were displayed on them. No company or personnel names.

No surprise, more greys were evident; the walls, maybe once a pale blue, but grey now, the floor too, covered with two-foot square carpet tiles from wall to wall, grossly stained with unknown substances. Some frayed, some worn badly, accidents waiting to happen. *How could anybody work here?* Michael wondered, considering unemployment an improvement on working in this building.

The seats were plastic with moulded bases that didn't fit the majority of bottoms. They were uncomfortable, unyielding and induced pain after a few minutes. Michael hoped the wait would be brief. Nothing worse than waiting, especially without magazines to browse through and stimulate a mind. Would this day deteriorate further or did hope wait behind door six? His answer was imminent, and he searched for a clock. Not long now, assuming the appointment would be punctual; so many weren't nowadays.

He found the clock, ancient, a relic from the 1970s with rotating digit cards. Twelve-ten it stated proudly, then clicked loudly as the minute digit changed from zero to one. 12:11, only nineteen minutes to wait.

He noticed others waiting to be called from those concealed behind the numbered doors. An assortment of old, young, tall, and short. This place made no discerning claim on who it attracted or what they needed. A click and the minutes changed to 12:12. Michael had heard of the Chinese water torture technique, where drips fell onto a man's head. Apparently, he would go insane waiting for the next drop. That it worked beggared belief, but now, waiting for the next click and rotating digit to change, he believed it could. Maybe this was even more powerful. The 1970s digit turning, torture treatment. Something for the Dragon's Den, perhaps. The thought of being offered cash for a percentage of his invention earnings, appealed, almost raising a smile. Click! 12:13.

Next to the clock was the date, Tuesday the fourteenth of December, on cards, that required manual change daily. Michael wondered which one of a procession of people, he'd seen working here, had the important job of changing it. Really! It's 2017, perhaps this place needed more than a physical makeover; it needed to engage technology too.

12:14 arrived with the proverbial click and Michael noticed he wasn't alone watching it; several heads turned to check. He wondered about their appointment times. Since his arrival, no door had opened, and no individual disappeared into the unseen offices beyond. But change was imminent. 12:15, door two opened. A voice called.

"David Mayhew."

A man stood, gathered his brolly and carrier bag and head toward it. He entered, it closed, and Michael never saw him again. 12:18, door nine opened.

"Beth Mullins," a female voice this time. Brusque and business like, cold and impersonal.

She rose and Michael watched as she limped apparently painfully through door nine. It closed and Michael never saw her again. He guessed another exit existed, if not, perhaps they met an early demise, courtesy of the Axeman, the latest serial killer being glorified on cable television.

And so it continued, people arriving and disappearing through opening and shutting doors, never seen again. The digits clicked repeatedly and now announced 12:42. His appointment long past. No surprise, nobody cared about punctuality these days. His parents obsessed about it, he and his siblings had inherited their views. What a shame nobody else had.

He sat there, lost in his world of nothingness, waiting for that infernal door to open. Door six, the only one that hadn't, typically it was his. 12:53. Finally, it opened, insufficient for him to glimpse inside. A slight pause before opening fully, his view blocked by the presence standing there.

"Michael Ferguson please."

Chapter 3:

Michael rose from his seat and head toward the doorway. *To boldly go where no man has been before,* he mused, quoting a line from a television show amongst his mother's favourites, a secret crush on William Shatner. A supposed secret that wasn't, everybody at home knew; though she was unaware.

"Follow me please," the suited man instructed, leading the way down a poorly lit corridor before stopping at the third door. He pushed it open, holding it against the spring-loaded hinges that fought to close it, and indicated for Michael to enter, pointing toward another cold, hard plastic chair for him to sit on.

The chair on the opposite side of the desk held no uncomfortable promise. Plush, black leather, complete with leather cushion and padded backrest. It swivelled silently as he reached for and inadvertently pushed it. *Now that's what I call a seat.* Michael thought, grimacing as his bottom connected with plastic. The man gently lowered himself into his chair and then made eye-contact with Michael.

"Mr Ferguson my name is Maxwell, Brian Maxwell, call me Brian if you wish; no need for formality here."

Looking into a pair of dark-brown friendly eyes Michael decided, instantly and totally irrationally, he liked this man; no, more than that, he trusted him. It was a bizarre feeling because he never trusted easily, and usually reserved judgement to liking somebody or not, until knowing them better.

"Michael, everybody calls me Michael," he responded, holding out his hand to shake the one that Brian offered. He didn't explain his mother called him Angel; not the sort of nickname to be shared liberally when you are nineteen.

"Forgive me Michael, while I find your paperwork, it's a failing of mine, I'm not in favour of it. There's too much nowadays, making everything formal and impersonal. I wouldn't want my clients being confined to meeting with a person mirroring that description."

"Maybe it would help if I told you what I needed, why I'm here," Michael offered, and Brian ceased shuffling the papers in his tray.

"Excellent idea, how can I help you?" he asked, displaying a perfect set of white teeth, appearing far too young for a man in his fifties.

Michael smiled back, he couldn't help himself, something about this man he couldn't quite discern; a calmness, a strong sense of peace, or something similar.

"Well, I'm here because I'm having trouble finding a job, I don't want to claim benefit, just help finding a job."

"Well, that's positive, plenty of jobs at the moment. The worst problems, for somebody your age, is lacking experience; youngsters want to change jobs the instant something offering financial improvement is advertised."

"Virtually all the jobs I've found on the internet, and in local papers, want experienced people, absolutely nothing to suit somebody like me. I apply for literally everything, despite the job and what they want."

"There are jobs available, but not advertised in the usual ways, a lot of advisors keep a few jobs aside for their clients and, as you are my client, you can access all the jobs I have. None of these are available to anybody else or advertised anywhere else. Most don't require qualifications, and are seeking somebody prepared to work hard and possibly forge a career."

He rummaged through his tray again and, against Michael's expectations, produced a small newspaper.

"This is a specialist paper covering a huge variety of jobs in your area. When you leave, consider this copy yours, work through it at your convenience."

Brian opened the paper and held it for Michael to see inside. It was packed full of career opportunities and job vacancies. He'd never seen a paper specialising in jobs quite like this before.

"Seven pages of jobs and I'll bet more than one requires a person like you."

"Wow! I didn't realise a paper just for job vacancies existed."

"People always need help occasionally. Now, you'll need this card. Every time you attend an interview, you'll be given a self-adhesive sticker by the prospective employer, sometimes two. Stick them on this card, even if unsuccessful; you can see where they need to be placed."

Brian passed over the card and Michael examined it. It was a standard piece of card, eleven by eight inches, and folded in half. On the front, and already completed, was Michael's name and address. Opening it, he found six boxes beneath the heading of location on the first page, and on the second, five boxes under the job title heading. Simple, with no frills. Turning it over, the back cover was blank. The simplest document ever.

"I know what you're thinking. It's not overly detailed? But it's popular with people in your situation, consider the time you've spent recently on the internet filling in forms taking thirty minutes each."

"All the employers have stickers?"

"Don't concern yourself with them, your interviewers understand my system and appreciate it, and as I suggested, some will give two. Plain and simple, in design, each has a letter printed on them. The letter is simply a code for the job you've interviewed for, and saves me a multitude of paperwork."

"That's it, that's all I have to do?"

"That's it, simple system, but gets results. When all the boxes are filled with stickers, I guarantee you'll have discovered a new place to work and a new career. Now, I'll write down my telephone number and extension on the back of your card. Any problems or questions don't hesitate to call."

Rising from his chair, Brian indicated the door and Michael understood the meeting was over.

"Any charge for the service, Brian?"

"That would be cruel, considering those I meet are jobless!"

Michael placed the card in the inside pocket of his jacket and picked up the paper. When Brian offered his hand again, Michael shook it warmly. Then he opened the door and led Michael back along the corridor.

"Have faith Michael, there's work for everyone out there."

"Thanks Brian."

Brian opened the door to the waiting room and Michael realised, unlike anybody else, he was where he started at. He glanced back before the door closed, but Brian had already disappeared. Crossing the room, he exited the door leading to the stairs. Two minutes later he entered the outdoor world, relieved the sun, though weak, promised something better.

Chapter 4:

Michael checked his watch, surprised to discover it was only one o'clock. Seven minutes, the meeting with Brian had taken only seven minutes, less if you considered the time taken to leave the building. The waiting period he'd endured, all for seven minutes of attention. *What's wrong with this world only affording seven minutes of help?*

It was hardly a meeting, instructions, a system to follow, possibly designed by a child, and the good wishes of a stranger. Still, he'd left with a paper full of jobs vacancies, but what type of jobs, jobs with a future, or dead-end jobs that offer nothing but the basic wage? Only a read could answer that, but after a year of constant rejections it didn't raise his expectations, or sense of hope.

Brian claimed there was a job for him. What did he know? Had he delved into Michael's skills, his qualifications, or a particular industry he wanted to work in? No! He couldn't even find his file. It told him a lot, and it told him nothing. Worse, he realised he felt no different than before the meeting.

He pulled out the folded paper from his pocket then opened it and checked the front page. Skim reading, he noticed none of the jobs required experience, and contained a mixture of full and part-time vacancies. They were limited in details but that didn't matter. What mattered was there were plenty.

Realising, he'd experienced his first positive thought of the day, he smiled. Something else too, he needed another cup of tea. What was it his aunt always said? *A cup of tea allowed time for reflection, and placed problems into perspective.*

The Wimpy was situated in the Lower High Street half a mile away from where he stood. Michael head towards it; a little more bounce to his step than earlier. Soon he walked through the front entrance, surprised to see it almost empty. Sitting down in a booth, he placed the paper down, picked up the menu and browsed through it. He wasn't sure why; he knew already he had barely enough change for a tea. Returning it to its stand, he waited for a waitress to serve him.

She arrived, bustling with energy unused on customers so far. She was short, slightly overweight, but with a pleasant face and engaging smile.

"Hello, you're my first customer in ages, what can I get for you?"

"Just a tea please."

"Coming right up."

She disappeared behind the counter and Michael glanced at his paper. He decided to wait for his tea before reading it. His father always read the paper with a cup of tea, so did his brother and sister, a family thing, a characteristic trait they all adopted.

He didn't wait long before she returned, and he pushed the paper to the back of his table, making room for his tea. At the last moment, she slipped, losing her footing and lurching violently forward. Michael's reactions were sharp, he reached out and grabbed her, preventing her from falling. The tea exploded from the cup, spewing out like an erupting volcano. Still gripping the girl, the hot fluid caught the back of his hand. It was piping hot and burned, instinct suggested pulling it away, but he couldn't release the girl. Gradually, she steadied, her face adopting a look of shock.

"Oh, my goodness, I'm so sorry, your poor hand, come, we should run it under the tap."

Michael rose, knowing her advice was sensible, if he didn't it would be sore for days. He followed her behind the counter. She took his hand gently, placing it under the flow of water. It stung, stung a lot, and Michael bit his lip, trying not to reveal how painful it was.

"How is it, any better, she asked, after a minute of immersion?"

"It's sore, but I won't die from it."

"I'm relieved, burns can leave scarring, and I was worried that might happen.

"It's not going to scar, so don't worry about that. Accidents happen and you didn't mean to slip."

"No, I didn't! Something slippery on the floor made me lose my footing. You saved me; I was heading for an awkward fall but you prevented it, you're very strong."

"It was instinct, I acted, no time to think."

"Well, I'm glad it was you; I mean I am, but I'm not! Oh dear, you know what I mean, I hope."

Michael laughed. "I understand."

"I'm Mary by the way."

"Michael."

The stinging subsided, and Mary carefully dabbed the water from his hand with a cloth. She examined it carefully, looking for signs suggesting further damage, but there were none.

"I think we've immersed this enough. There's a first aid box just over there, I'll check for a bandage to cover it."

"No need, it's improved, it's better left to the air."

"Are you sure? Ok, I'll clear the mess up and get you a fresh cup of tea."

She showed him to another booth, and he sat there nursing his hand, no longer putting on a brave face for her sake. Minutes later, she passed by, carrying a mop and bucket and something else in her hand.

"I'm really sorry Michael, but your paper is ruined. It soaked up most of the tea. I'll place it on the radiator, we might salvage part of it."

Michael stared at its condition. The paper had turned brown and dripping an excess of fluid it couldn't absorb. It was ruined, useless. His best chance of finding work, gone in an instant. *For Pete's sake, what else will go wrong today, why did I bother getting out of bed this morning?* he wondered. His face fell, he couldn't stop it, couldn't hide it and didn't want to; it really was the last straw. And par for the course his life had taken since leaving school.

"Oh dear, this was important wasn't it, I recognise the look on your face. I'm speechless, this is my third job in two weeks. I can't keep them, one thing after another, I'm so prone to accidents. No doubt I'll lose this one when the boss returns."

"This is your third job in two weeks? How do you do it, how are you successful at interviews? I've been unemployed a year, managed few interviews and never offered a job, and you've had three in two weeks, incredible."

Mary looked at the newspaper. "Oh, I see now it was full of jobs, that's why it was so important. The print is running, but we might salvage part of it," she said, moving off.

She returned in a few minutes with a fresh cup of tea. Michael feigned moving back in self-protection, and she laughed.

"You've been especially kind. Some customers would have created a heck of a fuss. I've put the paper on the radiator, it's boiling and should dry it fairly quickly. There are some bits unstained, so we might salvage some adverts. I insist on helping you with it; it's the least I can do. I break in half an hour. Usually, I go to the memorial gardens, but they'll still be wet, so I'll go to the library instead. Would you join me and let me help?"

"I could do this on my own Mary, I'm grateful for your concern, but I can manage."

"I want to help Michael, it's the least I can do, and I'll feel better for it, please."

"All right, I'll sit here until your break and then we'll go together."

"Thank you! I'll leave you for now, a few tasks I must do before the boss returns."

She disappeared and left him mulling over what had happened as he sipped at a second steaming brew of tea. *This age is confusing; I'm neither a man nor a boy; stuck somewhere between, yet facing the dilemmas of both? Life sucks!* he thought.

Chapter 5:

It was half an hour before she returned and Michael had semi-dozed for the past ten minutes. Thoughts running through his mind had overlapped in Grand National style and he kept falling at Beechers Brook; he had shut his mind down, focussing on the empty cup in front of him. It was a technique he had been practising for the past few months when his problems were preventing him from sleeping; he was getting becoming at it.

Mary appeared at his side from nowhere, fully donned with coat and knitted hat; his paper in her hand, or the remnants of it. It contained a mixture of crinkled and soft parts. Where she had folded it over the radiator it had completely dried but the top and bottom edges were still damp. Michael glimpsed the front page; it was clear there was little to salvage. The ink had run and formed a large ring, more accurately a blob. His heart sank, but he got up and followed her out of the café.

Outside, she started chattering about the weather, her grandmother and every other subject. Michael realised she was nervous, and this was her coping strategy. He wasn't sure how to quell her feelings, so instead let her continue, listening politely. As she talked, he admired her ability to say so much without taking a breath. He grinned suddenly; he liked her, the way she was, and how she spoke.

Her assessment of the conditions in the Memorial Gardens was accurate, still wet from this morning's downpour. Puddles littered the paths, and the grass looked squelchy. Typical for the time of year. So close to Christmas, it didn't feel like it this year. The town was quiet, more and more people shopped on-line to make savings. Mary didn't linger, and they hurried to the library.

Inside, she went upstairs to the quiet research area. Michael wasn't familiar with the room; he'd used the book areas for years, but never the research space. She selected an empty table, one of six set in a line, and sat down. Michael became conscious she'd stopped talking as she concentrated on separating the pages of the paper. She was careful and patient, teasing them apart, and he smiled when he noticed her tongue stuck out the corner of her mouth as she concentrated.

There were four separate sheets which she prised apart with no tearing; each had been full of jobs but Michael's heart slumped after realising they were in a complete mess. He looked away in disappointment and frustration.

"I'm sorry, Michael, but it looks like it's all ruined apart from six adverts. I'll get scissors and cut them out, it's no consolation, I'm sure, but six is better than none."

"I've a number for the man who gave me it, perhaps he'll have a second copy," Michael suggested.

Suddenly, a tear ran down Mary's cheek and landed on the paper. Michael noticed it and reached for her hand instinctively.

Holding it reassuringly, he spoke gently. "Hey, no need to cry Mary, I mean, come on it's only a paper after all, it's not worth crying over."

"It's not the paper making me cry, it's you."

"What?"

"You've been so kind; you could have been mean and called me names like fatty, but you didn't. I burnt your hand, ruined your best hope for work, and you've been kind to me. Few are like that these days."

"It was an accident, Mary."

"I know, but I keep having accidents, I keep losing jobs and I keep losing friends. Life can be so lonely sometimes."

"Why are you losing friends?"

"I make friends easily when starting a new job, but when they see how I'm accident prone I am, they lose interest."

"They don't realise what they're missing Mary. Consider your attempts to help me. It makes you candidate for friend of the year. I'd be happy to have a friend like you."

"I'd just be happy to have a friend."

"Well, you have one now, and while I realise that we didn't meet under normal circumstances, if we can move beyond this, we can handle anything. Let's leave here, go for a walk or something."

"I'm back at work in ten minutes, but thank you. I want to cut out these adverts first."

She busied the scissors and grouped the adverts into a small pile before giving them to Michael who placed them in his wallet.

"Thank you, Mary, I'll walk you back to work."

She collected the ruined remains and deposited them in a recycle bin, and they left. Back outside the sun had gone, and the clouds were massing again.

"Looks like more rain," she said. "I wonder if it'll snow this year."

"I doubt it, we always seem to miss it here."

"One day we'll get a white Christmas."

"One day perhaps."

Chapter 6:

Leaving her at the café, Michael walked slowly towards the town centre. He hadn't examined the jobs Mary salvaged, too late in the day to apply for them anyway. He'd examine them tonight, prioritise and make calls from home in the morning. His mother would witness his efforts and mention it to his father. He would know his son was still trying, hadn't given up.

A busker sat next to an entrance of one of the major High Street stores. Holding a tatty old guitar which had lost most of the lustre its varnish once gave it, he nodded to Michael.

The performer wasn't as easy to describe as the guitar. A heavily bearded individual with a shock of black hair hanging all over his face masked his facial features; but his hands, wrinkled and dry, gave evidence he wasn't young. Michael sat on one of the stone plinths circling a flower bed. He enjoyed listening to performers, admired their courage and their vulnerability in front of everybody, and he respected their passion for music.

Moments later, he strummed a few chords and a simple melody warming up. It was already chilly and Michael wondered how he kept his fingers flexible enough to play in these temperatures. The player suddenly eased into the first few lines of an Eagles classic. They were an old band, but Michael had grown up on the music of his parent's era. Take it Easy, was one of their major hits. He had a deep and decent voice, and Michael sang along with the chorus. For half an hour, he listened to versions of songs he mostly knew, before digging into his pocket and pulling out the last few coins he had. It wasn't enough to buy another tea, but Michael placed it into the tin the performer had positioned in front of him. He nodded his thanks as Michael rose to leave.

Moving away, Michael noticed the lack of people around, unusual so close to Christmas. Sure, the weather wasn't brilliant, but where was the Christmas spirit? A definite lack of it this year. Walking around the shops, he wondered if he would ever get enough money together to buy his family gifts, something else to fail at. He stared at a small, cuddly Santa soft toy. His sister would love that. She already had a collection of cuddly toys, making most shops look understocked. It was only £3.99 but it might have well been £399. He had nothing left, nothing at all. For a moment, his mind emptied, and he experienced a sadness wash over him.

Michael sat outside the council office block where he'd started his productive part of the day. Initially, it shocked him. One moment browsing in a shop, the next sitting on a bench with no memory of getting there. He hadn't walked; he was looking at the Toy Santa! How? What happened? A moment of panic and he felt for his wallet. Secure in his pocket, it was safe and the job adverts remained inside.

Michael felt another sensation, fear. Peering around the square, everybody stared at him as they passed by. The man carrying a briefcase, an empty expression, just a vacant stare. A woman with a shopping trolley glanced over, holding a stare for an unusually long time. A similar vacant expression adorning her face before she was replaced by a younger woman who stared openly. What was happening? Something else odd too, why weren't they wearing coats, it had been raining, and was mid-December?

Michael rose, intent on going home, feeling the need to escape. It was surreal and frightening. He'd never considered himself to be somebody who suffered from irrational fear, but he felt it now. Moving from the square to the High Street, he felt relief when most ignored him, as usual. The singer had stopped performing and glanced at him.

"You ok son."

"Yeah, I think so, thanks for asking," Michael said, without pausing from his stride. "Got wet from the rain earlier, just need home and a change of clothes."

"Grab a bath too, prevent the chills getting in your bones."

"Michael nodded and kept walking."

Half an hour later, he was home and relieved to find only his mother there. She fussed over him as she always did and ran a bath for him.

"Did you have any luck Angel?"

"Possibly, but for a bizarre accident at the Wimpy."

"What happened?"

"I'll tell you about it after my bath."

"They'll be a cup of hot chocolate for you when you get out."

"Thanks mum."

It was typical of her, always her children came first; it's what she lived for. Michael hoped he would be as generous with his time with his own children one day. The selfless acts so many mothers performed without a conscious thought. Could he match her as a good parent?"

Immersing himself in the steaming water, he soaked the misery of the day into extinction, smiling as he considered Brian and Mary's impact. Both had made a positive impression on him. Mary could become a good friend, he was not concerned about her accident-prone nature, as long as she didn't hurt herself or him too regularly. She was a kind girl who would help anyone in need. The way she responded quickly and responsibly to his burnt hand, suggested competence and intelligence, demonstrated further by her actions at the library.

Positive energy had finally emerged from a day. The first time for ages. He experienced a wash of optimism for a change.

Chapter 7:

Michael thanked his mother for the tea, settled back on a dining table chair and recounted the details of the day. He started at the employment office, not revealing the hours sitting on the beach, feeling sorry for himself. He was ashamed about feeling low, and didn't want to worry her; it wasn't his normal behaviour to show self-pity, not how he acted.

"You've had an interesting day, by the sound of it. I want to check your hand though."

"It's fine Mum, honest, not a mark on it."

He reached out, and she held it, turning it over, examining both sides before satisfied.

"Mary acted quickly and responsibly."

"Yeah, she did."

The kitchen door opened and Michael's father walked in. He nodded to his son and gave a half smile before reaching for his wife and kissing her lightly on her forehead. He did it every day without fail.

She smiled warmly in response. "Have a good day dear?"

"Same old, same old."

Her opening and his response, was equally routine. She affirmed her pleasure at his homecoming and he announced that working man was now home and in the guise of husband and father.

Michael's mood altered immediately, knowing what any conversation with his father would entail, it was inevitable, and would almost certainly become a full assault on him and his efforts to obtain work. Sure enough, he went at it true to form. "How goes the hunt for work, Michael?"

"Met a man who said he could help at the employment centre."

"And did he?"

"Yes, and no."

"What do you mean by that?"

"He gave me a newspaper full of jobs that aren't advertised anywhere else, but he didn't actually have a job for me."

"Have you phoned them yet?"

"Only just got home, it's probably out of office hours now. I'll ring them in the morning."

"Better to start now."

"I've been chasing jobs all day."

"You won't get a job sitting on your bottom here."

Michael suddenly saw red. His father goading him was the last straw, he couldn't take it anymore. A red rag to a bull.

"What the bloody hell do you think I do all day, every day? I don't sit on my arse doing nothing. For a bloody year I've filled in application form after application form, knocked on door after door, attended interviews chased after jobs I'm not suited for, or even qualified for, and all you do? All you do is push, push, bloody push. Back off and give me a bloody break."

Michael's mother raised her hand to her mouth shocked by her son's outburst. She had never witnessed him so angry, and knowing instantly he was close to falling over an edge difficult to return from. She opened her mouth to speak, but her husband reacted first. He too was shocked by his son's outburst, more annoyed by what he said than the cause.

Moving menacingly forward. "Don't you dare speak like that to me, ever, especially in front of your mother. Nobody swears in this house, do you hear?"

Michael's anger hadn't subsided and instead was rising to the point of being completely uncontrolled.

"I'm not a kid anymore. If I want to swear I bloody will, nothing you can do about it. All year you've been riding my bloody back and I've had enough. This isn't the 1970s anymore. In your day you could leave one job and find another the next day. Guess what dad, listen for once and hear what I bloody well say. There are next to no jobs. Do you honestly believe I want unemployment, no money, and no friends? I want to work; I want a job and nobody has tried any bloody harder to get one."

His father's face reddened as his own rose. "I told you not to speak like that to me and in front of your mother and you deliberately went against my wishes. Go to your room; stay there until you apologise to me and your mother."

Michael stood up quickly with a look of total disgust on his face. The chair flew backwards into the wall. His mother raised a hand and placed it on his arm, but Michael shook it off.

"Who the hell do you think you're bloody well talking to? I'm not a kid anymore and I won't go to my room. What bloody century are you living in? You're out of touch Dad, you live in cloud bloody cuckoo land. You go to your bloody room and consider how you've been treating me all bloody year."

Michael stormed from the room, slamming the kitchen door. His father rose from his chair but was stopped by his wife's hand on his shoulder.

"Let him go love. He's at a low point, I didn't realise how low until now."

"We have rules, a way to conduct ourselves. It's been that way since the birth of our first. None have ever acted like this. He can't get away with this. It's rebellion."

"No love, it's not, it's a cry for help and we should hear that, not see it as something different. Go to the working men's club, have a pint with the boys and I'll calm him down, talk and sort this out.

Michael's father stood up and there was still anger on his face. "Maybe I should. I'm angry, it will help calm me down."

"Think about what your son said darling, he's not exactly wrong."

"What do you mean?"

"You have pushed him hard."

"I've pushed them all hard, to make them strong, independent and capable."

"Michael's not the same as the others, he's a gentle soul, creative, caring. He's a little angel."

"No angel ever talked like that to his parents."

"You're taking it personally. Hitting out is a response to his situation, more accurately what's not happened. You've just taken the brunt, but it could easily have been somebody else."

"Ok, I'll leave it to you for the moment, but I will still expect an apology.

"You'll get it, this is Michael we're talking about."

Still disgruntled, he left the room, the front door closing quietly behind him. She left the kitchen too.

"Where are you, Michael?" she called.

Chapter 8:

The next morning, Michael sat at the kitchen table and removed the job adverts from his wallet. Selecting the top one, he started to read:

Wanted
Young person, male or female
To find homes for abandoned and unwanted pets.
Apply at the Ashley branch of the RSPCA.
Part-time vacancy only:

"Is that a job advert, Angel?"

"Yes, one I salvaged or, more accurately Mary salvaged. I'm really sorry about last night mum."

Smiling forgivingly, she touched his arm gently. "Leave that for now Angel, consider it more later; she sounds like a sweet girl."

"I think so, I need to speak to her before applying."

"Why?"

"The Wimpy is her third job in two weeks. That's amazing, she must have skills for handling job interviews to gain success like that."

"If you're meeting her at the Wimpy, you'll need this to buy a cup of tea, buy her one too, if she has magical secrets, we want to learn them."

She passed some coins across.

Michael smiled at his mother, she always understood his feelings, always forgave him when he wronged, and made him feel safer than anybody else in the world. They were especially close, and their bond special. Only his relationship with sister rivalled it.

"She'll like that, I know she will. She hasn't got friends; she makes and then loses them."

"Poor her, imagine trying to go through life at your age with no friends."

"I can imagine it mum, I'm experiencing that myself. All my old friends are working, they meet at places that cost money, like the bowling alley, or for a meal at the Indian or Chinese restaurant. I can't do that, and not finding work, it makes me feel I'm not as good as them, which, as they're all working, makes me the lowest of the low."

"That's rubbish Angel, there are jobs for you, and you're worth as much as anyone else. More to me! Now, take the change, buy Mary a cup of tea, make friends, and get that job, understand?"

"Crystal clear, mum," he said, rising from the table.

"And Angel?"

"Yes."

"Good luck."

"Thanks mum."

Michael strolled casually into town, pleased the rain clouds had passed. It was cold though, and he tightened the scarf around his neck. The Wimpy was busy, and he resisted entering. Talking to Mary could cause her trouble by preventing her working. She saw him through the window and came outside.

"Hello, I wasn't expecting to see you again so soon."

"Well, we're supposed to be friends, and I thought I'd offer you a cup of tea in exchange for information, but you're really busy."

"We are busy, but I get a twenty-minute break at eleven. Come in then, I'm sure I'll need a tea."

"Deal, I'll see you soon, now back to work before there's trouble with your boss."

With three-quarters of an hour to pass, he wandered up the High Street. The street performer was present again already into a session of eighties music. Michael didn't recognise the song he played, but stopped to listen, anyway. Excellent way to pass time. The performer recognised him and nodded a greeting without interrupting his singing. He finished and Michael clapped him.

"Seems like you're the only one listening today, thanks for the appreciation. You get that bath last night like I suggested?"

Michael grinned, "I did, my mother fussed over me like she always does."

"She's a good one your mum?"

"Do you know her; do you know me?"

"Oh, I meant that a good mum always looks after her kids without needing the smallest thank you."

"You're right there, and she is good, the best."

"It's good you recognise that. What are your plans today, shouldn't you be working?"

"I'm getting advice before trying for a job I'm interested in."

"Well, I wish you luck with that."

"I've got ten minutes before I leave, you going to play more?"

"You want to hear something specific?"

"No, anything, I'll like it."

"Fair enough."

He played solidly for the next ten minutes before Michael guessed it was time to leave. He raised his hand as he rose and walked away, receiving the nod he now associated the performer with, and strolled back towards the Wimpy. Reaching it ahead of schedule, he slid into a vacant booth. A different waitress served him this time, and he ordered two teas. Mary arrived just as the tea did.

"I'm glad you came; it's been so busy this morning I would probably have worked through my break if you hadn't."

"You need a break, Mary; everybody needs a break."

"Not much point when you spend it alone, reminds me of life outside work. At least at work, people need and talk to me, even as a waitress."

"Well, today you have someone to talk too. I wanted to ask you how you scored three jobs in two weeks; I've been unemployed for almost a year and haven't even got close. What's your secret?"

Mary smiled and edged a little closer. "Actually, my Gran gave me the idea, and it works almost every time. This job, I achieved through the interview process because my offer doesn't work with large, well-known companies."

"You've got my attention Mary, what's your offer?"

Suddenly, Mary's attention focused elsewhere, and she stood, as if to leave, before sitting again with a relieved look on her face. Michael turned to witness a woman tending a small and crying boy.

"Sorry Michael, I saw that child fall over on the cobbles outside. They are decorative, but lethal to the young and old who don't walk so well. I might have helped, but the mother is taking care of him.

"The magic is simple. I just offer to work for a couple of days free. A trial with a deal. If I do well, they pay and hire me, if not we say goodbye. Even I can get through two days without having an accident."

"Genius, absolutely genius. Why didn't I think of that, it's so simple?" Michael asked, a huge grin forming.

"Apparently, it was the done-thing when my Gran was young, everybody did it. It gave them a chance to try the job, to see if it suited, and it gave employers a chance to judge you as a worker."

Michael suddenly grinned at her. He suddenly understood why she spoke slightly differently from other young people. She lived with her grandmother. Her age group spoke differently, she spoke better, a little posh almost.

"Thanks Mary, I'm going for a job later, if it's good I'll try your tactic."

"Promise me, you'll come back and share how you get on?"

"Of course. I told you we're friends, and friends talk to each other. Mum says that's the way a trust forms between two people, if anyone knows she does, she still has friends from school."

"Wow, that's amazing. I can't imagine what that's like. My mum and dad died when I was young, a car crash nearly ten years ago now, I've been brought up by my Gran. She's an amazing person really, but she suffers from loneliness. Lately, she doesn't go out much; she's quite old and most of her friends have passed away."

A shadow passed across Mary's face showing Michael that despite being ten years ago she still missed her parents and lived with the pain daily. He couldn't imagine life without his mother and father and felt an empathy towards her.

"So that's why you speak differently, you speak like her! It's hard being lonely at our age, but for someone stuck indoors, it's hard to imagine how desperate she must feel sometimes."

"I'm company for her in the evenings, but during the day she's on her own; it's not healthy. She taught me to speak properly, but I've been accused of being stuck up, a snob and a posh twit."

"You'll have to take me to meet her sometime, I like old people, they have cool stories to share, having seen so much change during their lives."

"She has, to both, and if you're serious about meeting her, perhaps one night this week if you're free."

Michael suddenly felt a warm feeling as he realised the significance of the offer. She had affirmed their friendship; it felt good.

"Having no money means my social life is non-existent. Most of my old friends work, so I've plenty of free time. I'm re-thinking the type of person I want as friends too. Most of mine don't even call on the mobile anymore."

"You're right to reconsider them; if that's a typical example of your friends, you need new ones."

"I've started already with you, so we're both on the right track."

"I must return to work, but pop in and share how you get on. Oh, thanks for the tea, the next one is on me."

"Will do, your welcome, see you later."

Chapter 9:

Michael left the Wimpy and head up the High Street; it seemed he seldom went elsewhere lately. Considering the advice given by Mary, and the simplicity of it, made him shake his head. He was glad to have met her, and happy they were becoming friends. She had a positive effect on him. Even her accident-prone nature had proved positive; if she hadn't spilt his tea, they would have missed the opportunity to spend time together.

Veering into an alley running alongside the cinema, he immediately felt the day's chill as the high walls of the buildings on each side blocked the rays of warmth from the December sun. It was the eighth today, sixteen days until Christmas. The thought didn't change the fact he wasn't looking forward to it; still no money to buy presents for his family. The possibility of getting a job was bleak but not impossible, but would his new employer be generous and advance pay so he could buy the presents planned for each?

The sun snapped him back to reality as he exited the alley and started crossing the car park at the rear. A traffic warden, photographing a car whose ticket had expired, appeared dour. Where was his Christmas spirit? Why would anyone want a job causing misery to thousands? Definitely one he would never choose.

A screech of brakes followed by a yelp caught his attention. A man emerged from his car swearing loudly. He reached towards the front wheel of the passenger side and appeared to drag something away. Then, jumping back in, turned the car and drove away. Michael saw a dog laying at the roadside. He ran forward, recognising the form of a Labrador, but one laying unnaturally calm and still.

An older woman reached the dog before him. She used a stick and couldn't reach down without help. She was talking gently to the dog, trying to comfort the poor creature. Michael reached them both.

"You saw what happened," he asked her.

"I can't believe how callous and uncaring some people can be. He hit the poor creature with the car, got out, dragged it away and drove off."

Michael reached down, letting the dog sniff his hand.

"It's a Labrador, they're normally tame, but if he's hurt, and you touch a sensitive spot, he might react otherwise."

"Thanks, I'll be as careful as I can," he said, running his hands along the dog's back and then the tummy. No response and he checked each of the four legs and the tail.

"You're good with animals, gentle, caring. It has to be his head that hurts, you've checked everything else. I wouldn't touch it, too near his jaws for safety. He needs the RSPCA. They're just around the corner, less than a hundred yards away. Can you carry him, he's a big dog?"

"I'll manage, I was going there anyway. Thank you for your advice."

"You're a good lad, I hope they can help him."

Michael pushed his hands underneath the dog and lifted. Heavier than expected, he stood and started walking to the clinic. He didn't rush and talked softly to the dog for the duration. Reaching it, he realised he couldn't open the door and kicked it gently with his foot. Another pet owner with a patient, realising his predicament, opened the door and Michael staggered in, nodding his thanks. The receptionist asked him what was wrong with the dog.

"He's been hit by a car. I've checked his body over as best as I could, except his head, so that's probably where the problem lies."

"Where and when did this happen?"

"The car park around the corner ten minutes ago. I need to place him down, he's heavy and I've been carrying him for a while."

A door opened, and a man in surgical clothing appeared. "I heard the story, bring him in and lay him on the table."

Michael placed him down carefully.

"Well done lad, now wait outside while I give him the once over. What's his name?"

"Not a clue, he's not my dog; I just brought him here."

"Don't worry, take a seat, I won't be long."

The door closed and Michael remained standing. The woman behind the counter smiled. "Take a seat love and don't worry, he's a genius with animals, he'll sort this, and your dog will be fine."

"It's not my..." Michael started, and then didn't bother to finish.

He sat next to the elderly man with cage. Inside it, a large black rabbit sat hunched and still.

"What's wrong with your rabbit?" Michael asked.

"I'm afraid Cup Cake has an eye infection; it's constantly running and looks very sore."

"Cup Cake? You called your rabbit Cup Cake?"

"I'm a softie for rabbits, I just love them. I also love cupcakes; it seemed a natural choice."

Michael grinned. "You have a sense of humour too."

"Need that son, helps you get through life, it's tough out there."

"You're so right."

"What happened to your dog?"

Michael shared the story again, and the man listened carefully. "He's a beautiful animal, cared for, from what I saw, shouldn't be hard to discover the owner. They'll be posters up and all sorts of internet stuff and face book of course."

"Unless he's abandoned."

"Why would you think that?"

"That TV advert suggests a puppy is for life, thousands are disowned and abandoned every year."

There was an edge to Michael's voice that gave away the anger he was felt at the dog's plight.

"You seem pessimistic, if you don't mind me saying so."

"I witnessed a dog hit by a car, a man dragging it away and abandoning it. That's enough to encourage little pessimism. If not, try being unemployed for nearly a year."

"Good points, both, but life runs negative sometimes. Yours is just taking longer to turn positive, that's all. You'll get a break soon, I'm sure."

"Thanks, I hope so."

The door reopened, and the vet beckoned Michael to enter. Michael rose and followed. The dog now sat on the table and even wagged his tail.

"Wow, that's quite a difference considering he's only been here a few minutes."

"He took a knock to his head, still a little concussed, but he's improving nicely. I'll keep him here overnight to monitor, then wait until the owner gets in touch."

"What if they don't?"

"If not, we'll attempt to find him a home, but we only keep them for a short period. If nobody comes, and we're unsuccessful, he'll have to be put down."

Michael looked up sharply. "You're not serious surely, a beautiful animal like that."

"It's a hard fact of life, but we run on voluntary funding and don't have a bottomless vat of money."

"I can't believe this animal doesn't have a home, but if not, I'll find him one."

"The dog collar tab says his name is Charlie."

"Good, that's a help. No way is this animal is being put down."

The vet looked surprised at Michaels strength of conviction. The serious tone in his voice displayed his feelings and his determination. Few young men he met outside the treatment room displayed passion like this.

"What's your name lad?"

"My name's Michael. I was coming here to apply for the job you advertised, then this happened. I want the job. I'm prepared to work a week for free, so you can check out my work ethic. If I do good work, you pay me; if not, we say goodbye and no hard feelings."

"The job is part time Michael, and the pay isn't much."

"It's more than I've made during the past year."

"Ok, you've definitely got the passion for this, judging by your reaction. I'll give you the opportunity you want. One week for pay or a goodbye. When can you start?"

"When are you open next?"

"Monday's, Wednesday's and Friday morning; it's all we can afford to open for."

"I'll be here sharp for the next shift."

"Good, now it's customary to shake hands when striking up a deal."

They shook hands. "I'll see you soon, Michael, and please call me Bruce."

Michael grinned. "Thanks Bruce."

"Oh, and before you go, I have something for you."

He took out something small from his wallet and held it out. Michael opened his hand and accepted two pieces of card. "You understand about these?" he asked.

Michael stared at them in his palm, noticing each contained a printed letter. The first an E, the second an A. Reaching into his pocket, he pulled out his employment record card. Opening it, he placed it down momentarily and peeled the backing off the cards, revealing a sticky surface. He positioned them into the first boxes and pressed hard, he checked to ensure they stuck properly. Satisfied, he closed the card, placing it in his pocket.

He left and walked back towards the Wimpy hoping to share his news with Mary, but Mary had finished her shift and had left for home.

"I have work," he voiced, repeating his thought. It sounded amazing to say that.

Chapter 10:

After a quiet weekend, which Michael had spent avoiding contact with his father, he started work. He was given a tiny room at the rear of the clinic, equipped with a computer and laptop. With Bruce already taking care of his first customer of the day, it fell to Susan, the receptionist to show him the ropes.

"We've discovered the best results come from tackling every possibility simultaneously. For example, the dog you rescued yesterday, what we'd do is advertise it as lost through all the local social media sites, and advertise the dog as unwanted. Sometimes we never find the original owner, but we might discover a prospective new one, before the allotted time period expires."

"How many pets are put down in a typical month?"

"Depends on how good whoever does your job is, and how lucky we get. It's possible none some months, other times maybe a dozen."

Michael was horrified by the number of perfectly healthy pets having their lives ended prematurely. Finding homes for them had to be the preferred way, and today that responsibility sat squarely on his shoulders.

"Looks like I'll be working hard to decrease that number."

"Yes, but don't blame yourself during unsuccessful weeks, highs and lows in every job. There's a notice board outside in the waiting room where you can post images of lost or unwanted pets and a digital camera in the drawer."

"Cool, thanks, how many requiring homes now?"

"Two, but it could be added to during the morning shift."

"One's obviously the dog, what's the other?"

"A white rabbit, nicknamed Chalky."

Michael grinned at the name. "Ok then, leave me to it, and I'll start."

"Good, coffee break is at 10:30, I'll see you then."

She left, and Michael booted the computer. A list of addresses were taped to the side, which included social media sites, other RSPCA offices, and a variety of animal charities.

He opened the drawer and removed the camera, before walking to the rear of the building where the animals were kept. A separate enclosure, with a variety of cages and pens for different creatures. Michael saw the dog immediately, and it started panting as he approached.

"Hello beauty, good to see you're looking well," Michael said, opening the cage and petting the animal; it wagged its tail in appreciation.

"I don't need your picture because I know somebody who will absolutely adore you, but I have to take Chalky's picture."

He closed the cage door and pointed the camera to a stunningly beautiful and pure white rabbit.

"My, you are a handsome creature, I bet I can find you a new home before the shift is done. Now come on, pose for me; look at the camera Chalky."

"It's good to talk to the animals and show them affection, Michael. Good morning, and welcome to our little team of animal carers. Did I hear that you've a home already for the dog?"

"Good morning, Bruce, thank you, and yes I do, at least I think I do, but I'll need to take him for a ten-minute walk later to arrange it."

"No problem."

"I don't think this rabbit will be a problem either, he's gorgeous; the ladies in particular will fall in love with him."

"I think you're right; there'll be a cat coming in later, it's old and in my experience, the older the animal, the harder it is to place them. Its owner died recently. Do you think you'll like it here? We employ so many people for your position because it's a part time and low-paid, yet the personal satisfaction can be huge."

"I think I'll like it fine; I enjoy working with animals and the people normally associated with helping animals are decent caring people, the sort I want to work with. Perhaps long term, a little restrictive as a career."

"Well, we can discuss that later, it's good to have you aboard Michael."

Bruce left, and Michael returned to his tiny office and began advertising the rabbit. He found a taker in the first half hour. Taking a piece of A4 paper, he created a chart, listing a variety of animals to keep a record of what creatures he placed. Hopefully this would identify a pattern of which animals were placed easily which were difficult. After making the rough copy, he created a word document to replace it and then his own database to record the finer details of the creature and the homes they went too.

Next, he arranged for a pick-up time for the rabbit's new owner, and at tea break he asked Bruce if he should interview them to check their suitability. He learnt a system was in place to address that. A simple questionnaire designed to test potential owner's knowledge of the creatures they wanted.

After discussing the dog situation with Bruce, he learned he could pass the animal over to its intended carer, on the understanding if the original owner came forward, they would have to return it.

Michael took the dog just before eleven o'clock and head for the Wimpy, hoping eleven was Mary's normal time for tea break. It was, and she appeared outside the café when she saw him tying up the dog.

"Hello, what a beautiful dog, is it yours?" she asked, bending down and rubbing its head.

"Hi Mary, it's not mine, but I'm in charge of finding it a temporary, possibly permanent home."

Mary continued to pet the animal while Michael told her about everything that happened after he left her yesterday.

"People can be really horrible sometimes," she said, shocked at what he told her.

"The thing is, Mary, in our conversation yesterday you said that you and your Gran were lonely and this dog needs a home. Imagine the company for your Gran during the day, she'd have reason to go out and get exercise. It's a lovely way to meet others too, plenty of dog walkers around. In the evening, it could be company for you too. I kid you not, this dog is perfect for you both, it's placid, gentle and affectionate."

A huge grin erupted on Mary's face, and excitement about the possibilities caused her to shift from one foot to another. Michael noticed it. He grinned too.

"Michael, stop! I wanted him the moment you said he was homeless. You're absolutely right though, he fits the bill for all the things you mentioned and he's drop dead gorgeous. What's his name?"

"The name tag says Charlie, and he does respond to it. I have to do my best to find the real owner Mary but, if nobody comes forward in a month, he'll become yours. If I find them, you must return him, but there will be others."

"I want this one Michael, I want Charlie. Don't try too hard Michael."

"I have too, if he belongs to a child, how upset would you be if you lost your dog?"

"I know, I know, I didn't mean that literally."

"What time do you finish today?"

"Two o'clock."

"Good, I'll bring him to you then."

"I can't wait. Thank you, Michael, for thinking of us. You're a good friend."

Michael smiled, and then laughed as Mary gave him a hug.

"See you later."

Bruce congratulated Michael on his first morning's work and told him his trial period had expired. Michael looked at him disappointedly.

"No, you misunderstand lad, I've seen enough to know you're the right person for the job."

Michael's spirits soared, and his smile spoke more than his thanks. He collected Charlie, wished Susan a good weekend and, for the first time in months, he walked with his head held high and a slight skip in his step.

Chapter 11:

If feeling his improving situation wasn't sufficient for Michael, the smile on Mary's face boosted him further. She took the dog eagerly and hugged the creature. Her joy was like custard on his apple crumble. A magical moment, allowing him to feel positive about himself. He could not remember the last.

"I think I should come with you while you take Charlie home, Mary."

"Surely there's no need, he won't be any trouble."

"I agree, but I need to take my job seriously, and the responsibility of ensuring the pets I place like their new homes, is part of it. I plan to ask Bruce if I can set up an after placement visit for each, to check they, and their new owners, are happy."

"My, you are taking it seriously. I think it's a great idea and you can start with Gran and I."

"Cool, I wanted to meet your Gran anyway, this means I can do both. Charlie will be a great ice-breaker."

"You don't need an ice-breaker with Gran, she's a really friendly type, but I know what you mean."

"You normally bus home, but I suggest we walk today and give Charlie some real exercise; we can test him, see what he's capable of and how he responds, chasing sticks and walking with us."

"That sounds a lot of fun, and sadly, fun is often missing in my life."

"Me too, perhaps now we're friends, we can change that; make sure we have fun more often."

Mary smiled her agreement as they reached a crossing, then focussed on the dog.

"Sit, Charlie," she commanded. "Good boy," she praised, after his instant response.

"He's been trained well, Michael."

"That's good, but let's try him off the lead. If your Gran takes him for a walk, she won't be able to let him off, unless he responds instantly. We also need to see how he behaves around other dogs."

"You think of everything. I reckon the RSPCA have employed a real asset."

This time Michael grinned, as they approached the Prince Albert Park.

"We can test him out here, when we're well away from the roads."

"Sounds like a plan."

They continued walking to the centre of the park before Michael suggested stopping. He picked up a dead branch, fallen from an old oak tree, and snapped it into a sizeable stick before placing it in front of Charlie's nose.

"If you unclip the lead Mary and hold on to his collar, I'll throw the stick and we'll see what he can do."

Mary nodded and followed Michael's suggestion. Charlie remained sitting throughout. Again, Michael held the stick under his nose and then threw it. Mary let her grip relax and told Charlie to fetch, saying the word repeatedly. Charlie took off like a rocket, collected the stick, and returned it, sitting obediently in front of her and dropping it at her feet. She praised and petted him enthusiastically, and they repeated the exercise several times.

Next, they tried walking with him, off the lead. Mary kept him at heel for the duration.

"He's so good, Michael, especially as he's a young dog. He's been treated well and trained, it's likely his owner will come forward for him."

There was disappointment and worry in her voice.

"Can't be sure Mary, people get into difficulties, changes in circumstances force some to give their pets up. We had an old cat come in this morning whose owner had recently died. You can never tell, I guess what will happen, will happen; it's a matter of time. If Charlie has to leave, we'll find you another dog, I promise."

"Sorry Michael, he's so perfect."

"I get it, but for the moment he's yours, let's see how he acts with other dogs. There's one approaching us now. Carry on walking and keep him to heel and see what he does."

Charlie ignored the other dog who yapped excitedly, but otherwise didn't leave its owner.

"Right, one last thing to try. The next time he starts to sniff something, leave him and continue walking. When we get a distance away, we'll call him and see how he responds."

They tried it, and Mary called him once a gap of thirty metres opened up. He responded immediately, and they made a huge fuss of him before slipping the lead back on him.

"Time to meet Gran then," Mary said excitedly. "We live just down the road from the park."

Ten minutes later, they entered the gate at the front of Mary's home. She tied Charlie up outside.

Mary's grandmother was busy in the kitchen baking scones as they walked in. She greeted Mary enthusiastically and shook hands with Michael after Mary had introduced him.

"You're just in time for a hot scone young man," she said, smiling.

Michael told her he had worked up an appetite after his first shift at work and walking Mary home. Mary explained how they met at the Wimpy, and how decent Michael had been regarding the accident. Michael noticed how she had avoided saying anything about Charlie and was leading up to it in her recount of their activities together. Finally, she reached the part about the end of Michael's work today and informed her Gran there was somebody else for her to meet. She left the room and went outside to fetch Charlie.

"What's that girl of mine up to Michael?" she asked, her curiosity started to spike.

"You know there's never a dull moment around Mary," he responded, leaving the surprise in Mary's hands.

Mary appeared before she could say anything else, and Charlie trotted in behind. He went straight to the older woman and sniffed her hand affectionately. She was smitten instantly, just as her granddaughter had been.

"Oh, he's so beautiful, gentle and calm."

"And he's ours if you agree to it Gran."

"What do you mean ours?"

Mary explained what had happened yesterday and what Michael had suggested earlier in great detail. Her Grandmother listened to every word she said while serving the hot scones. Michael tucked in while Mary continued. When she had finished Gran looked at Michael with real appreciation.

"You're a really thoughtful young man, Michael. Few consider the elderly, seems most view us like out-of-date food, a nuisance taking space."

"That's not how I view anyone, Charlie needs a home, Mary needs new friends and you need company when Mary works. I've been unemployed for a year and I know exactly how it feels to be considered a waste of space. It's soul-destroying. Mary's advice helped me land a job, we've become friends and friends look out for each other."

"Charlie is going to help you get friends, Gran, too. As we walked home, people nodded greetings to us, one or two spoke, all because we had him with us. Dog walkers have something in common, obviously dogs, the outdoors and companionship. He's perfect for us. What do you think?"

"I think we'd better keep him then, and hope he was abandoned and nobody wants him back."

"Now that's all been sorted, it's time for me to leave. Thank you for the scone and hopefully I'll see you again."

"You're welcome anytime Michael."

Mary led Michael out and once outside thanked him herself. Then she gave him a hug. He wasn't expecting it, but it bolstered the good feelings about himself for the second time.

Chapter 12:

Strolling along the High Street, he stopped when noticing the busker performing again. He settled in the same location as before, listening to a rendition of Night's in White Satin. Curious how most of the singer's performances were his mother's favourites. He nodded to the man, who reciprocated. Reaching for his wallet, he opened it, and slid out another advert. He turned it over to read what it offered.

Shop Assistant Wanted
Male or Female
Flexible hours
Apply: The Tuck Shop
24 East Street. Ashley.

Like the previous advert, it was simple in design, failing to give any concrete details. Michael recognised the name of the shop; he knew it, having frequented it during his school years. The job didn't exactly scream career opportunities, but then neither did the first; it offered flexible hours. Could the work hours suit the gaps in his schedule with the RSPCA?

East Street wasn't far from his current location, five minutes' walk. Green Banks Secondary School was in the same road. There were two schools close by, and Michael had experienced the sporting rivalry between his school, Martial Street Academy, and Green Banks. Some of his former friends, attended there.

Most of the shop's trade came from children who schooled at Green Banks but Michaels own school, was close enough for their children to use it. With no other shops closer, it was convenient to avoid the longer walk into town.

Considering the job, the peak times would occur before school, during lunch times, and after school ended. It made perfect sense this was a part-time job, but he wondered what shifts were expected. Even if this job offered more money and hours, he wouldn't quit the RSPCA position. Deciding to visit before going home, it seemed a perfect opportunity to use Mary's tactic again, offer a free trial period.

He remembered the shop well, knew what it sold, recalled the narrow aisles full of sweets and crisps, and the small, packed chilled counter, holding a variety of sandwiches, pies and pasties. There were other basic convenience items, mostly tin foods, microwaveable two-minute meals, and general household products.

The bell on the door tinkled loudly as he pushed it open and entered, and again as he closed it behind him. A friendly faced man, in his late forties, appeared via the door by the counter's side.

"Good afternoon, young man, how can I help?"

"Nothing to buy, thank you, but I'd like to speak to someone about the job vacancy."

"That's interesting, I've had a few enquiring recently, but none as young as you.

The man's friendly face, warm smile, and startling blue eyes drew Michael's attention.

“What makes you interested in a retail position, most of my trade is from kids?”

“It could be a shrewd move to employ somebody young for the job, I’m not much older than the kids you sell to, and I know I’ve a good idea about the goods they’re likely to buy.”

“Makes sense, how else are you right for the job?”

“Well, I’m a good worker, always on time and I’m friendly with people.” Michael explained, enforcing his point with a smile. “The advert says the hours are flexible, what exactly does that mean?”

“I’m looking to expand my range of merchandise to make the shop appeal to a fuller range of customers. I want to sell dairy products, fresh fruit and vegetables, plus a small range of food items, as an alternative to the ready meal section I have already; you know, stock goods people might need urgently. The fruit and vegetables require collecting, daily and early from the wholesaler. Impossible to be at two locations simultaneously, hence the new position.”

“So, the job is for morning periods?”

“Yes, from seven to ten, fifteen hours a week, the pay isn’t brilliant, but it’s better than most shop work. Are you still interested?”

“Yes, I could fit it in with my other part-time job, if you were flexible.”

“Well, the interviews are taking place next Saturday. If you’re serious we can do the formal bit then. My name is David Jollie and you are?” he asked.

“Michael, Michael Ferguson,” he replied, taking the outstretched hand and shaking it. David’s grip was firm and Michael matched it, gaining an appreciative nod.

Further conversation was halted as the doorbell rang again and a young boy walked in and examined the extensive chocolate range.

"I'll book you in for eleven-fifteen on Saturday Michael and will look forward to seeing you then."

Thanking him enthusiastically, Michael started to walk towards the door. He'd achieved another interview and hadn't even offered his services on trial; he could use that strategy on interview day if needed. As he pulled open the door and turned for a final wave, he noticed the young boy reach for a chocolate bar and place it in his pocket. David didn't see him; his attention was focussed elsewhere. Michael exited and waited outside.

A range of thoughts rushed through his mind, presenting him with a dilemma. Should he report him to his school, should he march him into the shop and make him empty his pockets, or should he call the police? None of the options seemed wrong, but they didn't seem quite right either. He decided to wait until the boy left and decide after speaking to him; he didn't wait long as the door opened with the familiar tinkle announcing the boy's exit.

He appeared about twelve years old. A worried look suggested he carried the weight of the world on his young shoulders. For a moment Michael felt sympathy for him, why, he wasn't exactly sure. Looking into the boy's eyes, the younger lad couldn't meet the stare and immediately averted his.

"Shouldn't you be in school; best part of an hour before bell?" Michael asked, noticing the badge on the boy's blazer; Green Banks Secondary School.

The comment forced the boy to acknowledge him with eye-contact but he remained quiet.

"Which year group are you in, seven or eight?"

"Eight," the boy replied sullenly. "It's afternoon break, I snuck out to buy supplies."

"You mean steal supplies. How many things did you cram in your pockets without paying for?"

The boy's face fell and his shoulders slumped dejectedly.

"Who said I stole anything?" he asked, but with no indignant tone suggesting a protest of innocence.

"I saw you place a chocolate bar into your pocket as I was leaving the shop, and I suspect you have more."

"What do want, a share?"

"Of course not."

Running the options, he considered moments before, Michael remained unsure of which to take. The boy appeared to shrink, more than he had already, and then, as if reinforcing his observation, his shoulders slumped further.

"Let's sit and discuss this before deciding a course of action, maybe you'll have an alternative plan to mine."

Michael sat down on the kerbside and indicated for the boy to join him. He could have run, but made no attempt, and sat down beside him.

"So, why stealing? For need, greed or another reason?"

"I really wish you'd leave, pretend you never saw me, but that won't happen, will it?"

Michael shook his head, showing he agreed with his comment, and waited for him to talk. Questioning him hadn't produced a conversation starter yet, but he would need to leave soon; surely, he would talk. Despite that, the boy remained sullen and non-verbal, Michael realised he needed a different tactic to get him talking. He too stayed quiet, racking his brains, seeking a different way in.

Chapter 13:

The silence continued for a further five minutes before Michael realised he needed to break it. He was getting nowhere, but a sudden thought occurred to him.

"Somebody forced you into this, didn't they?" he asked suddenly, remembering an incident happening to a boy at his school several years ago.

The boy nodded, struggling to reply, uttering a quiet, almost imperceptible, yes.

"Not doing this means facing consequences?" Michael persevered.

Again, he managed yes before finally talking.

"I'll be late back; they'll know I'm missing and I'll get into more trouble for ducking out of school."

"Don't worry about school, stealing is more serious. Why don't you tell me everything from the beginning, what's at stake for you if you don't steal? You never know, I might help sort this mess."

"You reckon, do you? You don't understand what I'm caught up in, it's complicated, and other people risk getting hurt if I don't deliver," he said, his tone more than a little sarcastic.

"Like I say, you've nothing to lose by telling me."

The boy deliberated further before talking

"It started several months ago. I was seen in the shop at lunchtime, buying sweets with my sister who's in year seven. The group who saw us, stole our sweets, and the rest of our money. They forced us to give them our dinner money every day, and we're not the only ones. This group picks on loads of kids for this, hurting them if they don't.

"One day we didn't have money to give them and they told me I needed to do something else instead. If I didn't, they would hurt my sister. They gave me some coins to buy from the shop but I had to steal as much as possible so they could sell it at school, that's how it began."

"How long for?"

"Three, four months. I'm not the only one, they pick on other boys with sisters too."

"How old are the boys forcing this?"

"They're all year ten or maybe eleven. There's about eight of them."

Michael felt anger towards the group and compassion for the boy; he wanted to help.

"Do you know the names of other victims?"

He nodded miserably.

"What about the gang of older boys?"

"Yes, but I can't tell you because they'd find out it was me who sold them out, and hurt my sister, I can't risk it, she's small and done nothing wrong."

Michael nodded at his statement, not pressing him further. The boy was clearly scared; if he wasn't careful, he might refuse to respond.

"Still think you can help me?"

"Mm! There's always something to help, but you'll have to trust me, and probably tell your story to adults if you want this to stop," he said gently.

"I don't trust anybody anymore, and I certainly don't want to tell others about this."

"I understand, but while this continues the threat of harm to your sister remains, you don't need that worry on your shoulders?"

"She's my little sister, it's my job to protect her," he said simply.

"Yes, it is, but not with serious issues and threat of harm. You need help to deal with this permanently."

The boy considered it for a moment. "What would I have to do?"

"Tell me your name and we'll speak to the shop owner, he is a good and decent man. I'm sure he'll help; it's him who's being robbed because of that group."

His dejected look showed he recognised his lack of choice; he would follow Michael's suggestion, there was no alternative. "My name is Tom."

"I'm Michael, let's end this, Tom."

Standing up, Michael waited for him; he took his time, raising his body as if it were made of lead.

Michael sensed the fear coursing through him and his facial expression echoed it. He asked him to trust him and promised to see him through everything as he took the few steps forward. Michael pushed open the door, setting the bell ringing again.

"Hello, you're back, not changed your mind?"

"No Mr Jollie, I haven't but I've something very serious to discuss with you."

"And this young man, he should be in school shouldn't he. Is he a friend of yours?"

"Not exactly, but he does need our help."

"That sounds serious; right, you have my undivided attention, what's the problem.

"Right Tom, let's start by emptying your pockets."

Immediately, Tom took on a defensive stance and backed away. Michael placed a hand on his shoulder.

"Come on, consider your sister here."

By the time he had emptied the two pockets in his blazer thirteen different bars of chocolate and four packs of chewing gum lay on the counter.

"I'm sorry Mr, I had no choice, I didn't want to do it; really I didn't."

"I know you didn't Tom." Michael replied, answering quickly before Mr Jollie could say anything.

"Tell Mr Jollie the reasons behind this Tom or would you prefer me to?" he nodded, and Michael wasn't sure what he wanted.

A brief period of silence gave him a clue, and he relayed the story fully to Mr Jollie whose face got redder and redder at the injustice Tom had been experiencing.

"You poor boy, I can't believe this older group has acted so callously."

"He's not alone stealing; others are forced too."

"How many, Tom?"

"At least four."

Mr Jollie raised the closed sign.

"You're losing goodsworth hundreds of pounds," Michael said, reinforcing the scale of the thieving.

"That's not as bad as what's happening to these poor boys. Nobody should live in fear for their, and their siblings, safety."

"Don't worry Tom, this is what I suggest. First, I'll ring the head, he's a decent man and a friend. I'll ask him to come here right now. Then, we'll probably call the police and get them involved because this group need punishing."

"That concerns me, they might view it as Tom's word against theirs. Even if we find and persuade other boys to talk, there's no hard evidence to support Tom's case," Michael said worriedly.

"The police are no fools, and four boys complaining they're being forced to steal will add credit to Tom's story. I'll phone the head now. Michael, look after our friend, and mind the shop. The close sign is up, but the door isn't locked, somebody may enter. And Tom, don't worry, we'll get this sorted out quickly. You can be what you should be, a carefree schoolboy."

His call was brief, and he returned quickly. The shop door opened a few minutes later, and an older man with a friendly face and a balding head entered. He went straight to Tom and crouched down to the boy's height.

"Don't worry Tom, Mr Jollie has told me everything that's happened and we're getting this stopped now. The police will arrive too, but we'll need names of the other boys forced to steal."

Tom gave him three names, and the head asked to use Mr Jollie's phone.

"I'm going to bring the other boys here now; the police can interview all four together and then we'll call their parents. A tear fell silently down Tom's cheek.

"Do we really have to involve them, they'll think I'm a thief," he said miserably.

"I think they'll be proud of you for protecting your sister and understand you were forced to do this," Michael told him, and the head agreed.

The physical education teacher arrived with three more boys who understood instantly why they had left school, and recognised their shoplifting days were over. They glanced at Tom with worried faces, and the head told them to relax. He was putting a stop to the mess they were in. The PE teacher left, and the police arrived.

Chapter 14:

Two officers arrived, Constable Peters, a tall, strapping man with a stern face with a softer looking, and shorter woman, Constable Clark. The Head and Mr Jollie explained everything, sparing no details and the officers asked the boys a series of questions. Everybody was stunned to learn some had been stealing for nearly six months.

Asking the boys to name the older pupils, they reassured them there would be no repercussions. Tom originally believed there were eight, but eleven names were listed.

Constable Peters suggested with the amount of stealing happening, the older boy's lockers may contain stashes, as they probably sold the goods, at budget prices, at school to make money; not all would have sold.

The head asked how frequently they stole, and were told several days a week. He asked where and when Tom passed over the goods and learned he was to meet them outside the school gates after school.

"I'd like to catch them in the act." Constable Peters suggested. "If we could manage that, it strengthens the case against them, though I'm convinced we've ample already."

The Head agreed but wanted to call the boy's parents first. They needed to be informed and collect their children before the arrests were made. They also needed to make statements which Constable Clark would take care of at their homes. All the adults repeatedly reassured the boys that their parents would understand, and that no charges would be brought against them. Though still worried, they were displaying signs of relief that their torment was ending.

One by one the boy's parents appeared and took their son's home after learning what they had done, and why. Tom's father was the last one to make an appearance. Constable Peters took him into Mr Jollie's living area behind the shop to talk to him privately. When they returned the constable asked Tom if he was prepared to help them catch some culprits in action. Initially, Tom remained silent, but his father stated how proud he felt at the way he had cared for his sister.

"Finish this son. Experience the good in doing right."

Tom nodded.

It was agreed he would meet the youths, as previously arranged, after school. His task was simple, tell them he wouldn't steal for them anymore. The constables and the Head would hide in bushes next to the main gates; they would hear everything said. Mr Jollie asked to watch the proceedings, and act as an independent witness, and Michael offered the same. The plan was considered thoroughly, even the words Tom would use. Then the head took PC Clark to the school to check the youth's lockers. When they returned, they shared the news that each of the named eleven had numerous supplies of sweets and chocolates stashed and, combined, it was sufficient to start a school tuck shop.

End of school drew near.

Ten minutes before four, they walked down the street to get into position. There were already some parents present and Constable Peters asked them to wait a few yards further away. Then they crouched behind the decorative bushes, except for Tom, who stood alone by the gate waiting for the youths to arrive. Everyone was close enough to come to Tom's aid, if required, and would hear every word spoken during the interchange.

PC Clark would record everything said, her shorthand skills were apparently exemplary.

They waited and waited and just after five past the hour, Michael saw Tom stiffen as the youths approached. Five of them swaggering, totally confident, complacent with their next actions. They walked to Tom and surrounded him.

"What have you got for us today then Tommy boy?" one leered.

"Nothing for you today, or any day; I'm through with this."

One of the boys leaned forward and grabbed him by the neck of his shirt.

"We decide that, not you. I wonder if you will be so sure of yourself after we have done a little persuasion work on your sister, Lucy, isn't it?"

"You leave my sister out of it," Tom said angrily.

"For that to happen, you'd better visit our favourite shop right now or otherwise we'll persuade you; it will be painful."

"I said it's over," Tom stated, instantly recoiling after receiving a blow from a fist to the stomach.

Constable Peters emerged from the bushes and informed the youths they were being arrested for extortion and theft. His appearance stunned them, and they immediately proclaimed their innocence. PC Clark, the head, Mr Jollie and Michael emerged from their hiding places.

"I think you need to consider what you're saying carefully, boys. I've recorded everything said since your arrival and your Head also witnessed everything. The evidence is stacked against you, and the case will go to court," PC Clark informed them.

The boys were escorted back into school by the police, with the Head following behind, while Mr Jollie and Michael stayed at the gate. Tom's father took him home.

"You were good with Tom, Michael, I still can't believe he lived under threat of those youths for so long, the poor boy."

"Well, it's over now Mr Jollie, thank goodness and I hope Tom sleeps well tonight."

"I have something for you too, the latest chocolate bar from Cadbury's, everybody is raving over this, take it with my thanks, there's a couple of employment stickers too, you know about those don't you? I'll see you on Saturday."

Michael thanked him and began walking towards town. He removed the wrapping from the bar, suddenly feeling peckish, spotting the stickers on them. Peeling them off, he withdrew the card from his pocket. He opened it and pressed the two letters next to the others, an E and a V, before returning it to his pocket and taking his first bite of chocolate.

Michael had scored a great day, the best in a long time. Feeling good about what he had achieved, he strode back towards the High Street. He would have liked to have shared his news with Mary, but her shift had ended long ago.

The sun had disappeared, and the sky was darkening; time for home. He knew his mother would appreciate what he had done and couldn't wait to share the news. He veered off the High Street into an alley situated half way down it. It was a shortcut he often took when going home, it cut off the corner and the crowds when it was busy. Halfway down the alley, he heard footsteps behind him approaching fast. He turned and saw four youths, seventeen maybe eighteen years old. Two of them ran past him before stopping and returning. The others came towards him from behind. He was trapped.

"You're the pig that ratted out the boys from Green Bank School to the police aren't you."

"No, I helped stop young boys from being abused by those who should know better."

"So, it was you?"

"Yes, and I would help prevent anyone else becoming a victim like them."

"That's a problem, those you ratted on were our friends."

"I'd suggest looking for new ones. They'll be excluded from school, and punished by the courts, exactly what they deserve."

One of them brought a knee up hard against Michael's thigh, it deadened the leg immediately. He doubled over slightly and grunted with pain, and a second youth thumped him hard in the stomach. Michael gasped painfully, fighting for breath that wouldn't fill his lungs, and then a third boy punched him on the side of his head.

The world went dark for Michael and he slumped down almost unconscious. A fourth kicked his ribs, and they all laughed, until a shout from a man witnessing what was happening as he entered the alley, caused them to run off.

The man helped Michael to his feet and dusted him down as he spoke, seeking a reaction from him. Michael's eyes were opened and he started to focus again. He winced at the pain, pain everywhere, head, stomach, legs and ribs and moaned loudly.

"Easy lad, those thugs laid into you pretty badly. You might need checking out."

"I need to go home, that's what I need. My mother will know what's best to do."

"Do you live far lad?"

"Not too far, a five-minute walk, tops."

"I'll walk with you. Make sure you get there ok."

"No honestly I'll be fine, I just need to sit for a bit, back in the High Street, perhaps."

"Come on then lad I'll get you there."

"Thanks."

Michael hobbled to the High Street and sat on a bench, and after a few minutes, had placated his saviour sufficiently for him to leave. Feeling nauseous and dizzy, he regretted not accepting his help home, but he would be fine, he was convinced. He closed his eyes and relaxed, dozing a little, going in and out of sleep consciousness, never truly asleep, but not quite awake either. Flashing images forced their way into the depths of Michael's mind, powerful images, meaningful somehow, but failing to stir him sufficiently to wake.

Chapter 15:

Michael stood in a tunnel, covered in filthy-dirty ceramic white tiles, rectangular and small, unlike the squarer tiles in his bathroom at home. His movements were restricted, severely restricted, but he was moving forwards, by momentum, carried by more people than he'd ever seen in an enclosed space. He remembered a picture from a school history lesson depicting a bomb shelter in London, hundreds of scared people crammed in, fleeing the bombs falling above. Seemed more here! More even, than the one visit he had made to Wembley Stadium to watch England play football against the mighty Brazilian's; a treat from his father a few years ago.

Moving forward at a painfully slow pace, he wasn't even sure his feet took steps; it felt like he was hovering inches above the ground. He fought against the irresistible force propelling him forward, trying to prevent himself from pushing those in front.

The smells of such humanity were overpowering, ranging from the sweet perfume of a young girl to the pungent odour of sweat from an overweight man who had clearly been running, as perspiration covered his forehead in a light sheen. Another smell permeated the air, similar to the front room of a friend's houses, visited regularly before he left school and joined the army. Soot! Yes, definitely soot.

He had smelt it many times during the summer months when his family didn't light their old coal fire. He could almost taste it in his mouth. Feeling trapped, and claustrophobic, and with his personal space being violated on every side, he felt an unnerving sense of fear. He wasn't in control.

Then the disorientating noise, compounding his feelings further, a humming drone penetrated only by an occasional individual voice, as somebody exclaimed loudly at being pushed. A veritable sea of humanity, floating down the tunnel on a common course, unable to change direction or stop and defy the tide.

He saw a bend in the tunnel ahead. No, not a bend, a junction like the end of a road meeting another. He could discern the masses splitting left and right. Which way was he going; did he have a choice? He couldn't break free from the human chain that pulled and pushed at him and he would end up wherever they swept him, of that he was certain.

The images faded and disappeared and Michael sat on the bench in the High Street. He knew instantly had slept or had been unconscious, he couldn't be sure which. He checked his watch for the time. Nine o'clock! It was light! But that's not possible, it was almost five o'clock, home time. He remembered the thugs and the pain, but he didn't feel any pain now. Had he slept the night on the bench? It was cold, close to freezing, but he didn't feel it. Had he been home and didn't remember? No, that was ridiculous!

There were others present, there should be early morning, but... Yesterday was a Friday so it was Saturday now; the High Street should have market stalls, but there were none. So what day was it? Michael stopped an elderly woman just about to pass him by."

"Sorry, what day is it, I've got my days muddled?" Michael asked.

"Don't worry love, happens to me regularly, but today is Tuesday and it's Tuesday all day."

"Thanks."

"Merry Christmas."

"Same to you."

Michael tried rationalising everything that had happened. He remembered Friday's events clearly, he remembered feeling sick after being attacked in the alley, and sitting on the bench in the High Street. Then he remembered the images and the feelings he had experienced moments ago. He was probably imagining it, but he could swear he still smelt soot on his hands. The weird feeling from the tunnel experience wouldn't leave him, and the sense of fear remained. A familiar face loomed in front of him and a friendly voice spoke out.

"Morning lad, you're about brisk and early. If you were coming to listen to me then I hope I haven't kept you waiting too long."

Michael recognised the busker and grinned.

"Are you going to play something to cheer me up or chill me out?"

"What's your preference?"

"How about a cheer me up song?"

"Ok, I have a perfect one, it's guaranteed to cheer, but I'll take a few minutes to prepare and warm up. Why the low feelings?"

"I'm not really depressed but I'm confused over a loss of time."

"The older you get the quicker the time goes, that's a recognised and accepted fact."

"Well, the last few days have passed exceptionally quickly for me."

"Any luck with jobs yet?"

"I got a part-time job. It's really worthwhile with plenty of feel-good factor about it."

"Sounds perfect, so now you require a second part-time job to fill in the hours."

"That is the idea."

"Darn it, I've just broken a string, I'll have to nip to the music shop to get another. Keep up the good work with the job hunting and I'll owe you that song."

"No problem, have a good day."

"You too."

Michael checked his pockets and found coins in each. Not amounting to much, but enough for a tea. He walked towards the Wimpy. Mary! He needed the comfort of a familiar face. They were getting on well, becoming friends. Not just because of circumstances throwing them together, or rather throwing her at him, there was a mutual, genuine liking too, a comfortable companionship, and a shared understanding. He was walking the High Street again, how many times was that? He laughed at the unlikely nature despite the reality of it. Suddenly, he recognised it as a positive, it always led to someone he knew or was about to meet.

Entering the Wimpy, early morning, was positive too, rush hour had finished, those journeying to work had arrived at their destinations already; the onslaught of younger clientele, using the café to meet friends before school, had left too. It was nearly empty, and Michael found a booth and eased into it. It was the only café with individual booths, and Michael liked how it offered privacy. He saw Mary wiping down another table and raised his hand in greeting. She saw him and bustled over smiling.

"Hello Michael," she said, smiling warmly.

"Hello yourself."

"You went to investigate another job possibility on Friday, how did it go?"

"It was a bizarre afternoon and a long story, so I'll save it for later, but first, how was Charlie with your Gran."

"Oh my, Michael, it was almost magical, she hasn't been so happy for ages. The dog was lovely with her. They're inseparable already, and she's taken him for a walk twice a day."

"And what about Charlie and your loneliness in the evenings?"

"Well, I didn't feel lonely, Gran was more talkative, Charlie made a huge fuss of me, and I have a new friend who cares about everyone. It was amazing, if you suggested I'd feel this positive last week I'd have laughed. I don't have enough words to say how grateful I am, you've helped both of us."

"Well, you could demonstrate your gratitude by buying me a cup of tea, I can pay, but it would clean me out and leave me skint and penniless."

"You can borrow some from me until you get paid."

"That's kind, but any pay I get is for Christmas presents for my family."

"I feel like I've already had my Christmas presents, so it's only right I get you a tea."

"Thanks, and then when you have a break, I'll tell you what happened to me."

"Deal."

She brought him a cup and left him, and he watched her working. Visual evidence, suggesting she was happier, was clear, her whole demeanour was different. He was pleased, loneliness was a horrible, unpleasant feeling that could bring a person down lower than most emotions.

He considered the day ahead, and remembered the other job adverts in his wallet. A sober and worrying thought about his missing weekend and, most importantly, Monday. He had a shift at the RSPCA. Had he completed it, worked another day but couldn't remember it? He hoped so, letting them down would be terrible. The beating had affected his memory, either that or he still had a slight concussion. He also wondered about Tom. Had he negotiated the school day without being intimidated by the same group who attacked him. Perhaps he should call the school, warn them about a group exacting revenge for their *in-trouble* friends.

He decided and drew out his mobile phone. There was almost no credit left on it and, although he charged it religiously every night, he hadn't actually phoned, texted or emailed anyone for a month. He googled the school number and entered it, asking to speak to the head when reaching reception. The Head wasn't available, and he explained everything to the receptionist. Michael ended the call and put the phone away, hoping Tom, his sister, and the other young boys would have a trouble-free day. He'd done what he could.

Mary took her break early, sliding into the booth next to him with two cups of tea.

"You've been waiting for ages so you're due another cup."

"Thanks Mary."

"So, I have twenty-minutes, time for you to update me on everything."

Chapter 16:

Michael told her the story concerning the sweet shop, and everything that occurred there. She found Tom's, and the other boys, treatment shocking, wondering how anyone could be that cruel to another. She bestowed a non-stop barrage of praise to Michael about his responsible actions and caring way he had helped. Michael appreciated her comments, it raised his self-esteem further. He was at ease with her and their discussion revealed similarities between them at a deeper level. He was pleased they shared similar opinions and values. It made his next decision, to share the after events, easier. his beating and loss of time. Frustration mounted, realising her to return to work was imminent; he would have to wait.

He raised his hand to slow her exalted responses and explained his need to discuss something far more mysterious and worrying. She could sense his urgency and concern, and suggested they met during the evening. Michael explained he needed to see his father and make his apologies for the other day. She understood. Of course, she did, this was Mary, she understood everything, and that's why it was so important to speak to her, opposed to anyone else.

"The only possibility is after my shift. I finish at three today, you could walk me home, and still be home in time to see your father."

"Thanks Mary, you're every bit as helpful as you claim I am. This is important, discussing this with you is my only choice."

"I'm glad you trust me enough, Michael. For now, it's work, so I'll meet you at three."

"Three it is."

With three and a half hours to pass, Michael had a decision to make concerning what to do. No money left him with few options. He could pass time in the library, it was at least warm and dry, and he enjoyed reading. Perhaps window shopping for Christmas presents he could not afford yet. He opted for the library; it was only a two-minute walk from the Wimpy.

Once there, he selected a couple of books and settled down to read. He had not read for pleasure since his early days at secondary school, the fun of it spoilt by the constant analysing for hidden author meanings. He was convinced that most were invented for the purpose of a lesson. He spent the totality of time lost in the textual bliss of a good read, a million miles from reality.

Just before three, Michael walked back to the Wimpy and waited outside for Mary. The café had remained quiet, and she finished her shift promptly, smiling at Michael as she approached him.

"So, what's worrying you so much then, Michael?"

"I never said I was worried."

"You didn't have to. It was written all over your face. You're a little like me, you wear your emotions."

"I guess I do."

Michael relayed the events of Friday from being attacked by the thugs. Mary was shocked by his experience, and disappointed he had not informed her sooner. She scolded him slightly. After revealing the moment where he awoke, confused and disorientated, she exclaimed her concern.

"Sounds to me like you may have had concussion from your beating. It would explain the loss of memory."

"I was thinking along similar lines too, but I just can't accept it. I'd have remembered a shift at the RSPCA; I enjoyed my first there, and I had plans to discuss with Bruce. Going home would be difficult, I'd have apologised or at least spoken to my dad about my behaviour." My sister was coming home after two weeks away with friends, I was looking forward to seeing her.

"All these issues were important, possibly I might have forgotten one, but all? I don't think so. They weren't all negative."

"I understand why you're worried, Michael; I really do, but we can check out these things easily."

"How?"

"Simple really, you require a little patience. You'll work tomorrow, so you'll learn quickly if you missed a shift. You'll see your dad and sister tonight, if you'd been away from home since Friday evening, they'll have a barrage of questions about where you've been."

"I guess you're right, but I'm worried and I can't exactly say why, it's not a fear or guilt thing, but something else."

Mary stayed quiet, waiting for him to continue.

"Okay, we'll rest that a while, Mary, because more happened. Somewhere between Friday evening and this morning I had a dream, at least I think it's a dream. It was so real I can't be sure."

Michael shared the details about finding himself in the tunnel with a mass of humanity. He did not miss a detail, including his feelings. When he had finished, she refrained from comment while she searched for a possible explanation. Eventually, she spoke.

"Wow, Michael, that's spooky. Your descriptions and the sharing of your feelings made it seem so real. As real to me as it was to you. I don't have an explanation, at least one that seems plausible."

"So, what do you have?"

"It's as if your mind conjured up a story to counteract the pain you experienced, something more real than reality itself, if you understand what I mean."

"I do. But I don't understand the need. Yes, I had pain, but have experienced worse than the beating."

"What about the pain in your mind?"

"What do you mean?"

"Despite helping Tom, his experiences were horrible, your empathy for him showed in the way you acted. What if the pain from the beating, and your empathetic pain, compounded, making it doubly powerful? Sufficient for your mind to invent the story?"

"I guess… I can't be sure… No, I don't think so. I'm not convinced the dream or story are related with those events."

"In that case, I've nothing else to suggest. I'm sorry Michael, I've not been much help."

"I didn't really expect you to have answers. This was me sharing my experiences with you, so I don't feel alone with it. The worst thing I felt, when I woke on the bench, was isolation, being alone. I knew you wouldn't laugh or scoff at the story, and I knew you wouldn't try to dismiss it, like it never happened."

"I'm so pleased you confided in me. Of course, I wouldn't laugh at it. There's wouldn't be any point in you inventing this. You've done so much to help me; I feel disappointed I can't help you more."

"If you said nothing, listening without judgement was important. I'm relieved to have shared this."

"Well, I'm almost home, shall we sit in the park and talk more?"

"No, I should go home. I need to clear the air with my dad."

"Are you apologising for your outburst?"

"Actually, I'm not. I meant every word I said, but I said it in the wrong way. I'll apologise for my anger and the way I vented it, but what I said was accurate, and I intend to make that clear."

"Good for you, Michael, I think you're right after what you said before. Now, you're working tomorrow and my shift finishes before yours, so perhaps we can meet up on Wednesday."

"Sounds like a plan to me. Thanks for listening Mary."

"You're welcome."

They parted company and Michael started the long walk home.

Chapter 17:

Michael reached home half an hour before his father, giving him time to consider his approach. He worked the angles in his mind until they formed a massive tangle, and he opted for a head-on approach.

His mother and sister were visiting old friends, according to the note on the kitchen table. A casserole simmered in the oven for dinner. Michael realised he would be alone for dinner with his father, since his brother finished his shift at six. He started to lay the table, and brewed a pot of tea. Everything was prepared.

His father walked in at ten past five. He nodded to his son in his normal, informal way.

"Michael."

"Dad. Mum and Beth are out, and dinner's about to be served."

"Good, I'm hungry enough to eat us out of house and home."

He always said that. It was his way of showing appreciation for the prepared meal, but also his way of saying he was in husband and father mode. His friends, when visiting, often commented how different he was at home than work. He explained it by saying work and family had different needs, and he was right. He disappeared to wash his hands and Michael had served dinner and poured tea by the time he returned.

"Thanks son."

He always ate his dinner in silence, explaining it away by stating it showed respect to the cook, but Michael had other ideas today, it was time to reinforce his independence as an individual.

"I know you don't normally talk during meal times dad, but it's important we talk while we're alone."

"What's on your mind?"

"First, I want to apologise for the way I spoke and acted on Friday."

"That's taken a while, why?"

"I needed to mull over everything I said so I can be clear about what I'm apologising for."

"Fair enough, and that is?"

"Exactly what I said, for the way I spoke and acted. But not for what I said."

"Why?"

"Because I was right. You have been riding me hard since leaving school, you've been totally unfair."

"How so?"

"Like I said Friday, nobody ever tried harder to find a job than me. I listened to your words after leaving school, my choice, further education or work, simple, no third option like unemployment."

His father put down his knife and fork and stared hard into Michaels eyes.

"Apology accepted. And you are correct, I have ridden you hard because I don't want you to become complacent and give up."

"Giving was never an option, not for me. I chose work. I'm not academic, and the creative arts, which I'm good at, are difficult to earn a living at."

"Your choice was sensible, but the way you spoke to me, in front of your mother was unacceptable."

"I appreciate that, and apologised for it, but I want you to realise your behaviour to me is unacceptable too. If you said jump to me, I'd ask how high. I've never gone against you or mum ever. I'm nineteen now, and I'm not a child, and I know in your eyes I'm not an adult yet either, so that leaves me floundering in the middle. Surely, by now I've earned enough respect to be treated as a young man and no longer a child?"

"I don't express my feelings often, as you're well aware, it's a failing of mine, but you deserve it. You are not the same type of person as your brother and sister. Your mother is right, you're a gentle soul, and I should have been more sensitive towards you. I'm inflexible sometimes, another failing of mine, but it's a tough world and I don't want to see you swallowed by it, I want you to leave a mark. You recognise your weaknesses and can discuss them easier than I, and in truth, none of us are perfect, but I'll say this, and you'll know this for ever. I'm proud of the person you are, Michael, very proud. I don't want you to change or be the one who forces you to change. Yes, I want you to mature into a fine, upstanding individual, but I want you to be the type of man you want to be. So, I'm going to apologise for riding you so hard, with you it wasn't necessary; I should have realised that earlier, and second, I want you to understand how proud I am to have a son like you. Now, we should finish our meal and get cleaned up. When your brother arrives, and has eaten, the three of us are travelling."

"Where are we going?"

"London! The Hammers are entertaining United. It's high time we had a boy's night out. How does that sound to you?"

"Sounds great."

"One last thing."

"Yes."

"I'll do my best to treat you like a young man if you promise to tell me if I forget sometimes. Maybe I can learn from you too."

"Thanks, I appreciate that."

Ben arrived just after six and Michael instantly served his meal.

"The quicker you eat the quicker we're leaving. Dad's taking us to London to watch the Hammer's take on United."

"You're kidding me, what's got into him?"

"Nothing, he just said it was time we had a boy's night out."

"Happy days."

The timing was tight, but they arrived just before kick-off. Ben had insisted on singing *I'm forever blowing bubbles* for most of the journey and Michael and his father had laughed at his childish enthusiasm.

"I should have been harder on him, Michael. Twenty-three, and he acts more like an adolescent child than you ever have, where did I go wrong?"

Michael laughed, noting the pleasure and the pride his father was displaying. He seemed so relaxed, more than usual.

The game kicked off before they reached their seats and the crowd cheered. It promised much; two in-form teams near the top of the premiership. It would be a close game, and both teams had opportunities to score before United achieved it first. Except for one end of the ground, a silence prevailed. Disappointed Hammer fans adopted looks of shock and misery on their faces. Even

Ben fell silent temporarily before singing again and lifting the spirits of those around him. Others soon joined in.

"See that Michael, the power of positivity."

His father was right. He had ridden all his children hard and yet instead of squashing them it had inspired them to reach further, try harder and adopt positivity. He recognised himself in his brother, perhaps not as extrovert, but the similarity was there.

"I have it to."

"I know, and your sister. It's the one gift I wanted you all to have. To look into the face of adversity and be positive. All of us have that quality, Michael."

The Hammers started to attack the United defence with increased pace and urgency, there was only five minutes remaining. They won a corner and when the ball came across it was headed home by the centre-forward. The crowd erupted, a sea of claret and blue leapt, screamed and danced out of their chairs. Ben raised his tee-shirt over his face, dancing like a lunatic losing control.

"Did you teach him nothing about self-control?"

"I tried, believe me I tried," he said, laughing and joining in with the cheering.

After the game had ended with a draw, they made their way contentedly to their car and drove home. Ben constantly re-living every significant moment of the game.

"Bed suddenly sounds so peaceful, Michael, perhaps we should have gone to the game alone."

"We would have missed the *magic moments* and Ben's positivity."

His father grinned and remained smiling for the rest of the journey.

Chapter 18:

The following morning, Michael rose early, preparing for his shift at the RSPCA and deciding to surprise Mary with an early visit. His shift started at nine, hers at eight. He knew she would be busy with the early morning rush, but he could share how well his evening with his father had gone.

Walking into town, was different this early in the morning. People were different, on missions to reach work, school, or the shops before the rush. The pace of life multiplied compared to mid-morning or afternoon. Commuters, heading for the train station, elegantly dressed in suits and ties, while those aiming for the factories donning jeans and sweatshirts. The early morning shoppers were different. Any mode of attire was cool with them, not particularly concerned how they dressed.

Michael walked at pace. The air was cool and the exercise invigorating. The positivity from the previous evening still running high in his mind. But as he approached the High Street, he felt dizzy and unfocussed. He aimed for a bench to sit and rest, and reaching it, almost collapsed. His mind went blank, his eyes closed, and his world went dark.

The next moment, he opened his eyes again, or so it appeared. He felt a familiar disorientation. It had happened again, but without a dream or vision. He checked his watch, nine o'clock. He was late for his shift and had lost an hour. What was happening? Then he realised the day appeared different, it was sunny when he started out, but now it was grey and completely overcast. The temperature was cooler. A different day, not different weather. So what day was it?

Michael stopped an elderly woman passing by."

"Sorry, what day is it, I've got my days muddled?"

"Don't worry love, happens to me regularly, but today is Tuesday and it's Tuesday all day."

"Thanks."

"Merry Christmas."

"Same to you."

He recognised her from before, the words they spoke identical to their previous meeting. Losing days had happened again. Now what? He could visit Mary and tell her about it. But if today was Tuesday, was everything that happened yesterday a dream? He needed more information before sharing this with anyone. Another thought concerned him, was he ill, dementia perhaps or maybe a brain tumour, either could explain what was happening. People his age did not generally get dementia, did they, and tumours were quite rare?

He needed something to focus on. Mary could wait before he shared this. Likely, she would start believing he was having mental health issues. Possibly, it might strain their friendship and he would not risk jeopardising that. She was a friend worthy of keeping. He would pop in for a tea, greet her normally, but retain certain recent events to himself. He rose from the bench and started walking.

Reaching the Wimpy, he slid into a booth. Mary spotted him straight away.

"Morning Michael, tea?"

"Yes please."

While he waited, Michael reached into his pocket and pulled out his wallet. He opened it and retrieved one of the advertisements, and laid it on the table.

The format, the same as the previous adverts. Short and simple, with little information given.

Man or Woman Required
For
Physical Out-Door Work
Apply D. Brown
Ashley Cemetery

It sounded mysterious. Physical outdoor work, guaranteed, but what exactly?

Must be some sort of gardening, it's a cemetery after all, he mused. He could not think of an alternative."

Mary returned with his tea and spotted the advert.

"Another job to try for? Are you up for outside work Michael, you're fit, healthy and strong enough for it?"

"I used to help my mother with the gardening at home, I enjoyed it, didn't mind getting dirty. It was a hobby we shared. I enjoyed the time together and our discussions, about anything and everything. She joked we sorted the world's problems in the garden together.

"Will you research it, or visit on the off-chance?"

"Little choice really, these jobs don't supply a phone number just a person's name."

"You could get numbers from the Internet."

"I could, but my phone is low on credit and I need it in case of emergencies."

"Is it pay as you go or contract?"

"Pay as you go; I'll top it up when I get paid."

"It won't be long Michael; you'll have money."

"I've managed without it for so long, I'm used to it. It doesn't bother me like it used to."

"I must return to work, and you've a man to see about a job."

"I sure do Mam, and I'm leaving now, just got to saddle up my hoss."

"Idiot! Good luck, and let me know how you get on, I'm here until four today, and if you don't get chance later, there'll be a cup of tea for you here tomorrow morning before your shift at the RSPCA."

"Thanks, Mary. Say hello to Charlie for me if I don't see you later."

The cemetery was a distance from the Wimpy, situated on the town outskirts. If he'd had money, he would have taken a bus, but walking was the only option for him. The walk was pleasant, venturing this side of town was rare; there was no reason to, once passing the housing estate that expanded yearly, and now reached the edge of the Town Centre, you passed into open countryside which had a few large houses with personalised driveways and fancy names on wooden plaques.

Another thought of his mother crossed his mind. She said, if you were fortunate to buy one of these, you've arrived. It had taken years of listening to her before he'd understood what she meant by it. He counted seven of these houses on his side of the road before they ceased and the edge of the cemetery started.

As cemeteries went, this one was extensive, dating back to the eleventh century. From his approach, he could see several fields formed it, expanding over the years as demand for more space inevitably occurred. It was a beautiful, serene and a wide-open expanse, extremely well cared for and tended.

Typically, the entrance was at the farthest end, although short cuts through gaps in hedgerows existed. He decided to avoid them, knowing an old building near the entrance was used for storage and an office. The likelihood of anybody being there was slim, and he expected Mr Brown would probably be working somewhere in the cemetery, especially on a rain-free day like today.

Chapter 19

Approaching the entrance; two large columns of stone held enormous, ornate iron gates, pushed open and held in position by two huge bolts, disappearing into holes bored in the tarmac. Walking through, he knocked on the door of the building, next to one stone column. As suspected, nobody was present, and he followed the main tarmac path, meandering through the gravestones. A myriad of smaller, narrower paths branched off at different intervals, leading to groups of graves away from the main walkway. The grass in this section had recently been cut and the smell, like fresh bread or bacon, held that unique quality, bringing instant recognition.

Huge trees, oak, ash and chestnut, scattered the area, disturbing the uniformed manner the grave stones were placed in, and separating the vast area into smaller, discrete sections. It was beautifully designed, and Michael decided this cemetery would suit him, when his earthly existence was over. As he rounded one large tree, a majestic old oak, probably more than four-hundred years old dominated. He heard the humming of a small engine, guessing it as a ride-on mower like the council used on the grass verges and recreational areas. He was correct, two-hundred yards ahead of him, it was making progress across the direction he had walked. Changing course, he aimed for it.

Moving closer, he waved towards the driver, who returned the gesture but made no effort to stop his forward progress. He probably received plenty of similar acknowledgements during the day. It said hello, not stop so I can talk to you. Michael gestured again, and this time the man understood the veiled message and stopped. Switching off the engine, he left the machine and walked towards him.

"You need some help young man?"

He was younger than expected, with blonde hair and blue eyes, probably in his late thirties. He'd expected somebody older, perhaps he wasn't Mr Brown.

"I'm looking for Mr Brown, a Mr D. Brown." Michael said, and the man's ready smile told him he had found his target.

"That's me, but everybody calls me David.

"Hi David, I'm Michael, Michael Ferguson and I've come about the job in the advert."

"Oh good, few enquiries to date, although the ad hasn't circulated yet. I'm due for a break and a cup of tea, care to join me?"

This is different Michael thought before answering politely with an affirmative nod. David led him to a black painted iron bench, of which there were many scattered about at seemingly random spots. A small plaque held the words in loving memory of... Most of the benches had them, all donated by somebody who had lost a loved one, and who liked to sit at a particular spot close to their grave to remember them. David sat down and opened a small knapsack he carried over his shoulder and pulled out a small flask. Removing the lid, which formed a cup and held another, slightly smaller beneath it, he poured two cups of the steaming brew.

"So, you fancy being a Fosser then?"

Michael had no idea what he was talking about and for a second, was annoyed at his own ignorance.

"Sorry, the advert didn't specify the type of work, except it was physical and outside. David recognised his difficulty with the word Fosser and put him out of his misery.

"Lovely word Fosser, ancient, not used much today. I just love it though, sounds better than grave digger."

Michael hadn't considered grave digging!

"You're correct, the job description is lacking in the advert, but they're so expensive these days. I reckon the money is better spent on keeping everything here spick and span."

"It is a beautiful cemetery," Michael said warmly.

"The physical upkeep is relentless. There is only me, old Bert, a part-timer, and some volunteer gardeners since Alfie left and moved to Canada. The job, simply put, is basically gardening and grave digging, which we mostly do the old fashion way without using machinery. I need somebody reliable, hard-working, empathetic and respectful to the visitors here. Surprisingly, I've made many friends here during the years, even met my wife here. It's an amazing place to meet people, but you can't forget they're here to grieve. They need treating with sensitivity."

"Sounds like you've worked here for years, David?"

"I started here, at about your age, nearly twenty years ago, and couldn't imagine working anywhere else now. I would train the successful applicant to drive the mower."

In lots of ways, the job sounded perfect, physical work would keep him fit, and being outdoors in the countryside with the fresh air would be healthy.

"This sounds very positive David, when are the interviews?"

"I planned to allow the advert to circulate for a couple of weeks before checking the applicants. You've scuppered my plans slightly by coming informally; it's not a problem, I prefer to meet folks casually. Still need the formal interview to process the paperwork though, but after meeting you today, the paperwork becomes the sole purpose. What experience of gardening do you have?"

Michael told him it was something he used to share with his mother; David seemed to appreciate that, and then he played his trump card and offered his services for a few days trial.

"You are keen and, since I'm currently short-handed, I'd be interested in accepting that offer."

"How about Thursday this week, I know it's short notice but it's almost Christmas and you'll shut down for the holidays I expect?" Michael asked, pleased when his offer was readily accepted.

In his mind, he willed a word of thanks to Mary as once again her tactic worked. They shook hands and Michael left after thanking him for the tea. David head for the mower once more.

Michael smiled; weeks applying for jobs that proved fruitless, now suddenly he had gained three real possibilities.

He was feeling positive about himself again, not smug, but content with the knowledge his potential was being realised by others. Deciding to walk the rest of the cemetery before leaving, he started forming a mental picture of the layout. Enjoying the walk, especially the peaceful nature within the grounds, he appreciated having time to do it, although his situation would change soon.

Some of the wooden fencing, originally separating the individual fields, was in a state of disrepair and he made a mental note. Also observed, some of the older headstones required cleaning, and as he continued walking, he mentally recorded anything requiring attention. He would show he cared enough to want to maintain and improve the cemetery wherever he could.

At the furthest end, he noticed somebody sitting on a bench, the only person he had seen who didn't work there. She looked up as he approached, the saddest eyes he'd ever seen, peering straight at him. A half smile formed under effort. Michael returned the smile and said good morning. Impulsively, he sat down on the bench beside her. She pointed to the nearest gravestone with the immortal words 'In loving memory of...'

"My husband!" She said miserably. "He died six months ago in a car crash. I wanted to plant flowers by the stone, but I'm not strong enough to remove the roots that are everywhere."

A large ash tree stood defiantly, ten yards away, and Michael suspected the roots originated from it.

"Do you have any tools with you?" he asked. "I would be happy to help, if you'd like."

"Would you, that's so kind; it's difficult when you have one of these. Getting in and out is hardest," she said, pointing to the wheelchair he hadn't noticed, parked at the far end of the bench.

Chapter 20:

She reached out for the few hand tools concealed within a plastic carrier bag and offered them across.

"I was hoping to prepare the ground today and return tomorrow for planting; my mother's taking me to the garden centre later, when she picks me up. We're choosing perennials, saves planting every year."

He nodded his agreement, carrying the tools to the plot.

She pulled the wheelchair towards her and he watched as she awkwardly manoeuvred herself into it, before wheeling herself to the grave side. Michael wasn't convinced he should offer help and refrained. She proved she could manage, and he admired her determination and independent nature. Applying the lock on the wheels, she lowered herself onto the grass, bordering the grave.

"Sitting here is only possible when the grass is dry; recently we've had an abundance of rain, but it's dry enough today. If I remove the soil, could you cut the roots away?" she asked, and he nodded, watching for the first root to appear.

Attacking it with the trowel, he severed it at both ends of the small hole, and they worked for an hour before they finished removing the troublesome roots. As they worked, she introduced herself as Jennifer and shared a little about how her husband died. It was clear the pain of her loss was still raw, so he listened and didn't ask for elaboration, or questions, for risk of upsetting her. She asked about him and why he was at the cemetery today, and he kept his story brief.

"You must be frustrated not finding work, it makes you doubt yourself, makes you believe you're not as good as others with jobs. It's like when I lost the use of my legs. First, they told me I had an infection and not to worry about it, but as time passed by, they discovered the infection had attacked my nervous system, destroying key nerves transporting messages from my brain to my legs. Once they discovered that, it was clear I was unlikely to walk again. I remember how hard adjusting to life in a wheel chair was, but the difficulty finding a job was worse."

"Did you find work?" he asked.

"Eventually, two years of trying, I almost gave up, on so many occasions I knew my disability swerved employers away. Now I work for a charity helping others in similar situations as me."

Michael wondered where her reserves of determination originated from, twice the time he'd spent seeking work. He had almost given up, prior to this week. Achieving this after losing the use of your legs, Wow... Michael felt nothing short of admiration for her.

"That sounds like a rewarding job Jennifer. How long have you worked for them?"

"About five years. You're right, it's rewarding, but I don't see it as a long-term engagement

"What would you like to do?"

"I would love to write children's books, the illustrated ones. I'm good with art; in particular watercolour painting. I can invent stories about anything; I tell them to the children at Sunday school."

"So, what's stopping you, why don't you just do it?"

"Limited time, mostly. Work, other commitments, so little time."

"My mum says *having no time* excuses us from trying. I don't mean to sound rude, but if producing books is your target and makes you happy, make time, reduce some commitments to gain it."

"I have considered it, but my parents reckon I couldn't make a living from it from it. They believe I'm better suited to continue with my current job; the income is regular."

Michael considered his situation with his parents. His mother wouldn't mind him following a passion, if he had one, and would actively encourage it. His father, by contrast, would state the importance of finding a well-paid job, offering an opportunity to contribute to society. He understood her situation only too well.

"With respect Jennifer, surely what you do is your business, not theirs."

"That's true, but after Derek died; I couldn't manage my house without him to help, so I sold up and moved back to my parents. They are lovely to me but a little controlling."

"Have you tried talking to them like you've talked to me?"

"Yes, but perhaps not forcefully enough, they're pretty set in their ways and don't much care for confrontation or change."

"And you don't want to upset the apple cart, so to speak. They're good to you but still want to control you.

Sounds like a lot of older people to me." Michael suggested, and she nodded her agreement.

"When and where do you do your writing and painting?" he asked.

"Mostly, I do my painting at the weekends at home, but my parents insist I use the dining table, so the mess is not an issue; truthfully, I never make a mess. Worse, I can only use the table between mealtimes and if nobody else needs it. Having a timetable when you're creative doesn't work. You work when you're inspired, otherwise you don't produce your best work. As for the writing, I can write anywhere, it's something I can stop and start at will. I've written everywhere, and at the oddest of times."

Michael used to enjoy writing at school, and he got good grades in both English literature and language. Aware he had inherited his ability from his mother, his best work came when he was in the mood for it, at completely random times.

"That's the type of hobby I need, although writing is not the right choice for me. You need a studio or a space to adapt."

"That's a fantasy, or dream. It would allow me to pursue my painting without negotiating for time and space. The trouble is finding somewhere I wouldn't have to pay for; I don't earn great money at the charity?"

"I'm sure, putting our minds together, we might find some possibilities."

The sound of David's mower arriving threatened to drown out the chance of continuing the conversation.

"Sounds like we're going to have the peace shattered by David and his mower." Michael shouted, as he drew closer still.

"You've met David?" she asked.

"Yes, earlier, he's the one I spoke to about the job."

"He's a really nice man; everybody visiting here likes him because he always makes time for them."

Michael had liked him, too. He had a friendly and patient aura, and a ready smile. He experienced the same sense of trust in him as he had with Brian at the employment office. Again, he was surprised, he rarely trusted anybody so quickly.

Chapter 21:

David cut the mower's engine and walked across to where they sat.

"Hello Jenifer, how are you today? I see you've met Michael too. He came to talk about the job here, earlier," he said, his sentences all coming out in a rush in his enthusiasm to talk.

"Michael's been helping me dig out the roots that seem to multiply every time I plant something here."

"The roots belong to the Ash tree there," he said, pointing. "They've spread everywhere around this part of the cemetery," David laughed. "I bet it took you ages to clear them, didn't it?"

"I don't have the fancy machinery you have," Jenifer returned.

"True, that's true," he said jovially.

"What sorts of plants will you use? Please tell me you'll choose perennials?"

"As a matter of fact, yes! My mother and I are visiting the garden centre later to choose some."

"Well, perhaps I can help, I have a collection of plants remaining from the batch I ordered for the entrance display garden. If you like I could fetch a few and you could plant them today."

"That's really thoughtful of you David, thank you so much."

"Better than wasting them whilst I attempt to find somewhere else to plant them. I'll fetch them for you."

He jumped aboard the mower and rode off before she could say anything else, and returned after ten minutes with an assortment of plants on a large tray. They varied in size, flowered during different months, and their potential growth to full size covered a wide range. As Jennifer and Michael examined them, it was obvious her knowledge of plants exceeded his, and he decided to research a little before the job interview.

"Use whatever you need, and I'll return for the rest in half an hour," he said, placing them gently by the grave before walking back to his mower.

Immediately, Michael began passing them to Jennifer to read the names and position them on the grave. She placed the tallest growing plants nearest to the headstone and arranged the others so that they would taper off towards the end of the grave. He watched patiently as she moved them repeatedly until satisfied.

"This level of care with your writing and painting, and it's only a time before you've a best seller," he said, grinning.

"Patience, and attention to detail, is half the battle," she said, returning his grin.

Then they planted them, Michael dug the holes, and she set the plants firmly. They finished as David returned.

"I've brought water to bed the plants in," he said, examining the way the position of the plants.

"Clever, how the plants taper from the headstone, you considered this carefully. Would you like me to water them for you?" he asked.

"That's kind of you," Jennifer told him gratefully.

"I'm returning to the gatehouse; you two could benefit from applying water to your hands," he said, indicating the muddy state they were in.

"Drop by and freshen up when finished. It's cold water, but it's better than none."

And then he was gone once more. Jennifer asked Michael to help her into her chair and he lifted her gently. They wandered slowly towards the gatehouse. David greeted them as they arrived, showing them to a sink inside his store room.

"This is a lovely old building, David," Michael remarked.

"Dates back to the sixteenth century. I use most of the bottom floor for storage and a make-shift office; the upstairs has been unused for years. Shame, a house needs life within, even if attached to a cemetery."

An idea emerged in Michael's mind. The thought forced a grin, he hoped they would be impressed.

"David, I know how to achieve that regularly.".

"How?" he asked, with a curious expression.

"Jennifer wants to become a children's book author and illustrator. She's an excellent painter but has nowhere to work. It's holding her back from achieving her dreams. She writes anywhere and everywhere, but with painting she needs somewhere with space and plenty of light. I reckon one of the rooms here would make a perfect studio. It must be a downstairs space for access. What do you think?"

"This has possibilities. There's a disused kitchen, completely stripped out, except the sink unit. There are old sideboards upstairs that would create storage for your materials. All you'd need is a table, and comfortable chair. They're liable to be upstairs too, a lot of old furniture remains there. I could give the space a lick of paint to smarten it. It lacks heating but you can buy old Camping gas heaters for peanuts these days," he said excitedly.

"That's a great idea," Michael added.

"Wait a minute, before you two map my entire future, I need to have my say," Jennifer laughed.

"Of course, sorry I got carried away, David said, feigning remorse, but failing dismally.

"I would love to accept your offer, but I insist on helping sort out the room, and decorating it."

"Working on a project together will be cool Jennifer, let's inspect the space."

The room was perfect, and Michael decided to leave them sharing ideas. Jenifer called him over and asked him to lean forward before hugging him. She thanked him for the help and the inspirational idea and, last, for the confidence in which he showed in her. David shook his hand again and reminded him about next week, then he gave him a packet of sweet pea seeds which Michael had mentioned earlier were his mother's favourite, to take home with him.

Michael returned his thanks and left them discussing decor and paint. As he walked through the gates and head back towards town he inspected the seed packet, noticing something taped to it. He peeled it off, noticing a sticker on the reverse side. Pulling out the card from his pocket, he mounted the letter N alongside the others. Strange how they appeared in strangest places.

He planned a stop at the Wimpy to share his day with Mary, as promised. Musing about all those decent and helpful people he had met recently, he wondered why everyone couldn't be like that, world over. Great things happened when people worked together and showed care for others without strings attached. Mary would definitely enjoy this story.

Michael checked his watch. Still early, he could check out another advert. If he continued this way, he could be offered more jobs than manageable. Considering it further, he realised the difficulty in choosing which ones to accept. The choice was unnecessary for now, and he needed time to check out those in his wallet.

Passing the houses his mother admired, he was in town again before he knew it, and with his mind on other things, he almost walked past the busker who still owed him a song. He called as Michael became level with him.

"Got your mind on other things lad, have you forgotten I owe you a song?"

Michael grinned. "Sorry, I was miles away."

"I could tell, is everything all right?"

"Everything's cool. Another positive interview, so things are improving."

"That's great lad, positive things happen to considerate people giving more than they receive."

"How do you know I'm that sort of person?" Michael asked curiously.

"I always know a good person when I meet one. Do you want that song yet?"

"No, actually I'm suddenly feeling nauseous, I better sit down for a while." Michael said, his face adopting a paler shade

"Stay close by, perhaps my songs will lift you."

"They do, even when I don't feel rough."

"That's good to know, take it easy lad."

Michael walked towards a bench and sat down heavily. He seemed to worsen by the minute. As well as nausea, his head pounded violently and his body felt drained. He closed his eyes and groaned.

Chapter 22:

Michael was back in the tunnel of dirty white tiles, swept along with the surge of humanity. Again, the sense he couldn't control anything attacked his confidence, and, approaching the junction, something snapped inside his mind, wanting to prevent his forward travel.

Panic swept through him, and he attempted to turn. He succeeded, but there was nowhere to go. Hundreds of people, walking, pressing him further and further towards the junction. He fought, trying to force his way past two business men in grey suits. They walked, side by side, in the same predicament as him but without the panic. He couldn't pass them and they ignored him completely, as if he did not exist. The flow forced him backwards, like walking against a hurricane.

Michael attempted another change of direction, sideways, heading towards the young girl with the perfume. She was smaller, easier to brush aside, but in this tunnel, she was an immovable tank and the relentless movement continued.

The panic inside increased, and he fought his way past, pushing against her to lever himself into the tiniest of gaps behind. She didn't even notice him. No, more like she didn't even see him. Where was her response to his physicality? What was happening here?

He had manoeuvred past one, but was getting ever closer to the junction. Using his hands, he tried to force an opening between the two men behind him. They parted, but instantly another filled the gap he'd created. There was no escape, his efforts lessened as he tired, and finally gave in to the inevitable. He twisted around and peered ahead at the junction, ever closer; the feeling of dread intensifying. He closed his eyes, trying to erase it. The sounds changed, the smells vanished, and a breeze of fresh air caressed his face.

Opening his eyes, he found himself on a bench, but a different one; once more outside the employment building.

He felt an all too familiar disorientation. A repetition of events, within a dream or vision remained embedded in his mind. He checked his watch, nine o'clock. It had happened again?

The weather had altered, a mixture of cloud and blue sky, and a struggling sun, blinking its presence in the gaps. The temperature was similar. A different day, different weather! So what day was it?

Michael stopped an elderly woman passing by."

"Sorry, what day is it, I've got my days muddled?"

"Don't worry love, happens to me regularly, but today is Tuesday and it's Tuesday all day."

"Thanks."

"Merry Christmas."

"Same to you."

The unemployment building made him shudder. The cold, stark, nature of it compounding the memories and feelings from his visions, and he needed to escape from it. He rose and started walking towards the High Street, passing the busker belting out another old rock song from the past who grinned at him between words.

Aware he no longer felt sick, he also realised the pounding in his head had ceased, too. He continued down the street, heading for the Wimpy, the promise of a cup of tea and the friendliest of faces. But despite feeling physically better, his mental health required a boost.

Mary saw him arrive and beamed. He was glad she served him, still unnerved by his latest vision. Visions, seemed a better word to describe them than dreams, nothing else seemed appropriate or right. It wasn't a dream, he was convinced. He had never experienced a dream twice or one moving forward in time. It wasn't real, couldn't be. Impossible to be in two places, here and in a tunnel.

For a moment his thoughts returned to his first vision, and smelling soot on his person. He sniffed his arm, it was there, feint but there. No, it was impossible. He was here, in the present, exactly where he should be.

Sliding into a booth, he failed to quieten the feelings of unease. Mary would break soon; he definitely needed to share this. She would listen, he knew.

She brought a tea over, instantly realising something was wrong.

"I break in ten minutes, started at six this morning, a kitchen deep clean," she said gently.

She recognised his need to talk, and he hadn't said a word. She was already his best friend; he trusted and could rely on her. He smiled, thanking her for the tea, but the smile didn't hide his concern and Mary sensed it again. She touched the back of his hand.

"I won't be long, Michael."

Sipping at the scalding tea, he was glad it was so hot and burnt his lips slightly. He needed to shift his feelings and the sting of the burn helped.

He'd almost finished it when she returned with a second cup.

"I'm thinking you're psychic," he said, smiling.

"What's happened Michael, why so edgy. Did something happen at the cemetery?"

Michael explained the events of the morning leading to the point of sitting on the bench. "Great, you had another positive interview then."

"I did, but it became weird after."

"What do you mean weird?"

"Well, you know what I told you about losing my memory of the past few days and I saw visions, images of a tunnel."

"Yes!"

"Well, it happened again."

Michael shared the details in full, and she shivered when he described his feelings. He didn't hide the extreme panic, experienced in the tunnel from her, or his attempts to escape from it.

"My goodness, that's spooky, no wonder you looked freaked out."

"It's more, Mary, whatever lies at the end isn't good, I'm convinced. I was wondering if I'm having a premonition, seeing an event that hasn't happened yet."

"Surely not Michael, the tunnels you're describing don't exist around here, and you've no money to travel anywhere, which makes it impossible."

You're probably right. But I tell you it seems so real."

"Do you need to speak to someone?"

"I thought I was."

"Not me silly, a professional, someone who understands visions or dreams, or whatever you're having."

"I don't think so, it's already helping talking to you."

"Well, that's positive, I reckon. Something to focus your mind on will help. You know what I'm thinking don't you?"

"Wouldn't be another job advert, would it?"

"Now, who's the psychic one?"

Michael reached into his pocket and drew out his wallet. Opening it, he took out another advert and placed it down on the table.

Do you know your sport?
Are you physically fit?
New career openings in sport training
Apply T. Macham.
Ashley Sports Centre.

Mary read it out, word for word.

"Wow, this could be perfect Mary, I love sport, am good at most."

"You'll be trying for this, then."

"Too good to ignore."

"I suggest finishing your tea before walking down there."

"You know I consider you my best friend Mary, despite not knowing you for long."

"You're mine too, Michael, and I'm glad we've managed that."

Michael finished his tea. "After Christmas, when I get my second payday, I'm going to take you somewhere nice for tea, somewhere with huge slices of cake and scones and stuff."

"I'll keep you to that."

Chapter 23:

The sports centre was situated beyond the town centre, a mile and a half from the Wimpy. He decided to walk, attempting to retain the positive momentum of the past few days. Taking the alley, leading to the Memorial Gardens, he skirted the town centre, opting to take the Station Avenue approach. Although a lengthy, and straight road, trees lined it on both sides, adding life and colour. They softened the geometric harshness of the drab, three-storey office blocks, erected on both sides of the road.

Michael often wondered why a town as small as Ashley needed the volume of offices it contained, but had never discovered the answer. Half way down the avenue he took a left-hand turn into Summerfield Lane. The sports centre, with its impeccably manicured, extensive grounds, stood towards the end. Once a frequent visitor, playing five a side football, he was familiar with the entire complex.

As usual, a small queue, mostly young people, dressed in a multitude of sportswear, paused at reception before entry. Waiting patiently for his turn, the pretty receptionist smiled at him, before he reached her. She said good afternoon, asking him what sport he wanted.

"I'm came to see T. Macham, although I'm not sure if it's a man or a woman, about new career openings," Michael told her.

"It's Terry, and it's a man," she said helpfully. "He's taking a class in the badminton hall, which finishes at two. You're welcome to wait here, or enter and watch if you prefer."

"I'd like to watch, please."

"No problem, do you need directions?"

"I know where it is, thanks."

She pressed a button and the turnstile lock released, allowing him to push through it. Climbing the steps, leading to the viewing area, for most of the sporting arenas, he walked to the far end that overlooking the badminton hall. The glass window was smeared, covered with hand prints from those observing previously, but the view was clear. Four courts in total, but only two currently in use.

A man and woman occupied one, laughing at their bungling attempts to hit a shuttlecock, missing it completely more often than not, and Michael couldn't help smiling at their efforts.

On the second court, four men took their sport more seriously. He watched, admiring their skill and ability. A fifth man in a red sweatshirt, with the sport centre logo, stood coaching them. From his position, he could see the coach was young, probably in his twenties, but his features were blurred by the smears on the glass. He watched the game for ten minutes before deciding to walk to the hall and use the seats at the side to watch further.

The match was totally enthralling, the men were good, and he listened to the coaching Terry gave. Clearly, despite his young age, he knew exactly what the players needed. They listened too, and acted, on his advice, often winning the next point. When the game finished, they shook hands and head for the changing rooms.

Terry stayed behind and, using a large, cloth-covered broom, with a wide head attachment, mopped the court, removing spots of perspiration fallen during the game. Michael made his way across to him.

"Mr Macham, I'm Michael Ferguson and I've come to talk to you about the career opportunities in the advert."

"Hello Michael, call me Terry, everybody calls me Terry. So, you're interested in becoming a sports coach. What sports have you played, and how's your knowledge on sports you haven't played."

Michael listed the sports he had played and told him honestly that he understood rules of most sports he hadn't.

"You don't have to play sports to coach them, although it helps, especially with the tactical side of the game. Here, let's hit a few shuttles, see what you've got."

Terry passed him a racket and a tube of shuttles and selected a racket for himself. It had been a while since Michael had played the game, so he took it cautiously, ensuring he hit the shuttle sweetly before trying harder on direction and power.

Terry ran him all over the court, but Michael spotted a pattern to his shot selection and predicted where the shuttle was going. He forced Terry to retreat to the back of the court by increasing his power and then hit a softer shot, barely clearing the net before hitting the floor.

"Well done," he grinned. "That was a great last shot. Follow me."

Placing the racket down, he led the way out of the hall and along the corridor toward the squash courts. A feeling of self-doubt about his ability shot through Michael. He had never played squash. Fortunately, Terry led him past the courts and toward the table tennis rooms.

"I'm the only table tennis coach here at the moment and, although it won't be the only sport the successful applicant will coach, it's one of the most important considerations."

Asking him if he had played, Michael answered yes with confidence. At school, there was a table in the common room and he was among the best of the players. What a stroke of luck he thought. It wasn't long before they were into a long rally, taking it in turns to play defence whilst the other hit smash after smash. Terry was good, but Michael held his own and after ten minutes they stopped. Terry asked him where he had learned to play and who taught him. He was surprised when Michael revealed he had never taken a lesson.

They talked about the other sports Michael had played, asking him about his ability. It didn't worry him when Michael admitted little experience at some. Terry talked about courses Michael might be expected to attend, should he be successful, some courses taught how to play, and others taught coaching techniques. Finally, he asked if Michael was free for the next hour, pleased when he received an affirmative answer.

"The thing is Michael, I have a lad coming in to play table tennis in ten minutes," he said, glancing at his watch. "Now, I've seen your capability with a bat, the question now is can you coach? The lad is good, better than me, better than you. I'm playing him and I wondered if you'd stay and test your coaching ability.

Nobody is perfect and, despite his talent, you can spot faults or weaknesses from the side lines, a player might miss while playing. What do you reckon, prepared to try?"

Michael decided quickly, he had nothing to lose. He wasn't a trained coach, but anybody can give advice if knowledgeable enough. And he knew this game well.

"Yes, I'll give it a go," Michael told him, and then they continued to hit a few rallies while waiting for Terry's opponent.

On time, the door opened and a young man of Michael's age walked in. Terry greeted him warmly, introduced him as Lee, and asked him to warm up with Michael. Michael wasn't expecting that, but would enjoy taking part. He decided to use the warm up routine used at school with his friends.

"Let's start with close table rallies, forehand first and then backhand, followed by offensive and defensive rallies and finish with serving." Michael said, trying to sound like he knew what he was doing.

Lee nodded, and they were straight into very high-speed, close, table rallies. He hit the ball harder than Michael expected, and incredibly low over the net. Terry was right, Lee was good, and it took him several moments to adjust to his speed and power before he kept the rallies going with credibility.

The offensive and defensive work was similar to what Michael had experienced with Terry, but with the exception they focussed concentration on forehand and then backhand. He hit the ball harder than Terry too, and had amazing defensive skills, far superior to his own.

When serving, Lee threw the ball high in the air and kept his bat out of Michael's vision to conceal the type of spin, until the very last fraction of a second. At first,

Michael's defensive returns did not allow for the spin of the ball; it fizzled off Michael's bat in the opposite direction from intended, missing the table completely. He grinned, marvelling at the skill, until frustration set in and he concentrated harder. On his ninth serve, he anticipated correctly and smashed the ball beyond his reach.

"You learn quickly," Lee said.

"I need to against an opponent of your calibre," Michael told him. After the warm up, Terry took his place at the table, stating he had held his own admirably.

During the first six points, Michael remained quiet, looking hard for a weakness in Terry's game he could get Lee to exploit. Terry was good, but not at Lee's standard, but he soon noticed a weakness with his backhand on defensive strokes away from the table. When they changed ends, Michael told Lee to put more attacking balls to Terry's weaker stroke and Lee won the next five points straight.

Terry looked at Michael with a little frustration of his own.

"You advised him well, but now I'm behind, what's your advice for me?" he asked.

Michael smiled. "Keep him at the table, play to his backhand on his serve because he's slow getting into the central position and serve to his backhand because he doesn't return the ball as ferociously as his forehand

Terry promptly won the next four points to trail just two behind. Lee looked at Michael with mock dismay.

"I thought you were my coach," he said, grinning.

"Surely, it's a better training session if the game is closer, and you have to apply different tactics."

"True, very true!" he said, grinning.

Terry lost the set by four points, and Michael continued to coach both. Terry won the second by the narrowest of margins, but could not win the final. They both congratulated Michael for his observational skills, and Terry was pleased because he had taken a set against Lee for the first time. Clearly, as far as table tennis went, Michael had showed his potential as a coach.

"For a young lad with no experiencing of coaching you showed that you have some real understanding of the game and how to exploit the weaknesses of players engaged in it. Well done, Michael." Terry said, grinning.

"Yeah, thanks Michael, you were right, keeping the game close made it far more enjoyable," Lee told him.

Chapter 24:

With the match over, Terry told Michael to consider himself semi-interviewed. While admitting his approach was unorthodox, he had learned more about Michael than was possible in a conventional interview set up. There was still paperwork to consider, and he had several other candidates to interview; a final decision would be made Friday week.

Walking back to reception, he gave Michael an application form from the receptionist, and asked him to complete, and hand it in before leaving. Michael was in a buoyant mood, everything had gone positively well, and he considered the possibility of becoming a trainer. Potentially, this job carried more career opportunities than the others so far. He returned the completed application form to the receptionist and the girl smiled and wished him luck.

Outside, the sun was still shining, and he adopted a more leisurely pace back towards town. He hadn't travelled more than ten yards, and still within the sport centre grounds, when he spotted Lee. He was freshly showered and sitting on a bench by a small decorative garden at the entrance. Michael stopped when close enough to talk to him.

"You play a mean game of table tennis, Lee," he told him enthusiastically. "Do you play in a league or competitions?"

"Unfortunately, both, my whole life revolves around table tennis," he said, and Michael noticed the word 'unfortunately,' mirrored in his facial expression.

"Why unfortunately, I would love to have a talent like yours."

"While that's true, I doubt you'd like the life it offers, unless table tennis was all you cared about."

Michael sat on the bench beside him, asking what he meant.

"Since the age of ten, my dream was to be was a teacher. I had a male teacher, during my last year of primary school, who taught me that being a disruptive child was not the way forward if you wanted to achieve your ambitions. I didn't learn it straight away, but he spread the message through the disciplines of table tennis. I was a real pain in the backside then. I thought being disruptive, messing around, being defiant, disobedient, refusing to work, or anything resulting in the wrath of the teachers was cool. Cool in the eyes of other kids.

Michael was surprised, it was not what he expected. Even though he barely knew him, he understood having skill at a sport to Lee's standard, required work, a lot of work and self-discipline.

Lee continued. "Whilst I didn't gain any popularity with the staff, it did wonders for my street cred, I was every kid's hero, I lost count of the times I received detention or got expelled for days at a time. During my last year, Mr Harcourt threw me a lifeline and introduced me to table tennis. He taught me the strategies of the game, how to win and lose gracefully and, most importantly how to achieve goals by working hard at something. I won the district under eleven title, the county title, and came third in the national championships the following year.

"I wanted to be him, a teacher specialising with difficult children. I continued playing table tennis because he supported me, even after I left school and until he moved away to New Zealand."

Lee paused and Michael asked a question.

"How does playing table tennis prevent you from becoming a teacher?"

"That's a long story," he said pausing, and Michael waited patiently for him to speak again.

"Up to the time before I met Mr Harcourt, I wasn't only considered a bad boy by my teachers. My father lost patience and continued to show little interest in me for several years. I was a waste of space, unworthy of being his son, believe me I'm not exaggerating. Without my mother, I'm convinced he'd have been physical.

"Anyway, after I won my first competition at district level, he showed interest again, started turning up at my training sessions with Mr Harcourt. Mr Harcourt believed it was positive, that he seemed so supportive, he let him help organising various local competitions I was competing in.

"My father pushed hard and entered me into competitions in older categories and, although I did win a few, he was disappointed when I lost. He used to rant and rave behind the scenes whilst acting differently around Mr Harcourt; it made me try harder. The misery in his eyes was evident. It's difficult living up to your father," he said, pausing.

Michael nodded, understanding exactly what he meant. His father had never experienced unemployment, held the same job for twenty-five years, and was more driven than anyone Michael knew. He was unfaltering in the manner he conducted himself, and of the expectations he placed on his children. His momentary thoughts ceased as Lee continued.

"I applied myself similarly in other studies and finally become a straight-A student at secondary school, gaining all the qualifications needed for college or university. I wanted to become a teacher. When I told him of my choice of career, he went ballistic, stating it was a waste of time, long hours, few prospects, and lousy pay. I should stick to the table tennis and make millions from sponsorships and advertising deals, after becoming a national champion and a British sports star."

"Potentially, you could do both, have a sporting career first, then teaching afterwards, most sporting careers are usually short."

"I considered that, as a compromise, but table tennis is not what I want. I love it as a sport, and how it makes me feel. It's a constant reminder that sport can help the under privileged, or needy. A focus to help them choose the right path. I don't want my future centred around a bat and ball and who can challenge me. I want a life where the bat and ball assist me, and challenges others to make positive choices. Can you understand that?"

"Yes, I can. My dad wasn't interested in me staying at school either, said it was a waste of time because I didn't achieve the top grades. What really mattered was working, working hard, getting noticed and achieving promotion."

"How did you feel about that?"

"I wasn't a straight-A student, not even a straight B student, so perhaps he was right. In your situation, you can choose whatever career you want."

"Except, being a teacher; in his view, it wasn't enough. I'm not allowed to seek employment, I finished school two years ago and have never worked. I train daily; he claims he's making the ultimate sacrifice by allowing free board at home, instead of me contributing."

Lee fell silent, his eyes staring unseeingly into the distance, and Michael felt empathy for him. He hadn't paid his way either, considering that didn't aid his current positive feelings.

The conversation ceased, and they shared a quiet period of companionship on the bench. Michael realised little he said would improve Lee's mood, but he felt compelled to try. He thought about how important Mary had become, as a friend, who he could unload his worries and concerns on, and how she didn't judge him. He wanted to offer the same to Lee.

"You're an adult. You decide on a chosen career, nobody should do that for you," Michael pushed, hoping to restart the dialogue.

"He said if I quit competitive table tennis and follow another career he'd disown me, especially as I owe him for years of support."

"You're in a difficult situation, but have you asked yourself which scenario is worse."

"What do you mean?"

"Well, what's worse, playing table tennis against your wishes, or being disowned by your father and pursuing teaching?"

"That's easy to answer; the direction I'm going in is worse than being disowned by a man who loves bragging about his son, as a potential national champion."

"In that case, leave home and go to university," Michael said emphatically.

"I'd need money to do that."

"So, get part-time work, find a bedsit, it's for three years, offer your services to a school teaching children table tennis, like Mr Harcourt did. You can earn money, and practice being a coach."

Michael paused, allowing Lee time to consider what he was saying. He struggled to look positively at the options, focussing on the negatives.

"It's not as simple as that, I'd lose my family."

"Do all your family feel the same as your father?"

"No, my grandmother thinks teaching is a good career and my aunt and uncle."

"Would or could they help you with somewhere to stay while you get sorted."

"My grandmother possibly, no probably."

"That's where you start then, because you've already shown you can achieve when you apply yourself and work hard. When you're qualified and earning more than your father, he'll probably start to realise you made the correct choices, and that he can't live his life through you.

Terry said it's easier to notice things when you stand back, easier than when involved. He was right? You have two choices; either you're a table tennis star or a teacher, one choice will make you miserable, the other happy, the rest is just details. I talk to my elder brother if I have a problem. He says things are only a problem if you let them be, he's the happiest person I know, nothing ever worries him."

Lee looked thoughtful as if contemplating everything, and Michael respected that, he had said enough already. They sat quietly for several minutes before he broke the silence.

"Are you going to take that coaching job if it's offered to you?"

"I'm definitely interested," Michael replied, the change in subject suggesting that they had talked enough about his problems.

"I know you impressed Terry when you told me his weak spot, and you sure found one in me, too. Maybe if you get the job we can hit a few balls together, I'll tell Terry that he's getting too old and I need younger blood to prey on. That'll make him laugh for sure. I'll put in a word for you."

"Thanks," Michael grinned, "and I'll definitely help you practice anytime, job or no job."

"Where are you off to now?"

"I've got two more jobs to apply for, so I'm heading into town."

"I've going to meet my girlfriend shortly, so we could walk in together."

"Sounds good!" Michael said, rising from the bench. They strolled gently towards Station Avenue.

"So, about this girlfriend of yours, Lee, what's she like, does she have a best friend?"

Lee laughed, "Judge for yourself when we arrive; she has plenty of friends, she's a popular girl," he laughed.

She wasn't there when they arrived, and Michael decided not to wait. They shook hands vigorously.

"By the way, I have something for you," he said, reaching into his sports bag and pulling out a table tennis bat. I have loads, don't let Terry pass you off with one of the sports centres bats; they don't perform like these, especially if using spin on the ball. Thanks for listening to me earlier, believe it or not, you were a great help."

He passed Michael the bat who thanked him for his generosity and then left him there. The plastic bag covering the bat was unsealed, and he drew it out to examine it. The rubber covering was incredibly smooth, thicker than the one he played with earlier. Lee was right about using this one for spin. On the handle were two stickers an A and an H and Michael peeled them off. He pulled out his card from his pocket, sticking one on the left side, completing all the boxes available, and placed the second on the next. *The stickers keep finding unusual ways of getting into my possession,* he thought, as he returned the card to his pocket.

Following the shortest route for the rest of the journey, using alleyways between roads to save walking the lengths, he decided to return to the Wimpy, and tell Mary about his afternoon. He hadn't used her tactic this time, but still needed to share his positive news, after weeks of frequent disappointment.

Chapter 25:

The restaurant bustled, few available seats remained, but the booth he used before was empty, and he slid in. There were several waitresses on duty, more than earlier, probably part timers used to cover the rush hour periods, but there was no sign of Mary. Another waitress arrived to serve him and he ordered his customary cup of tea and asked after her, learning her duty finished an hour ago. He felt a pang of disappointment and decided to return the following morning to share his news. Perhaps he would have more to tell her, after investigating the remaining adverts.

The tea arrived and Michael added extra sugar, enjoying the sweetness on his tongue as he swallowed. Nothing beat a cup of tea. The inventor of this drink had discovered success for sure; tea was available everywhere. He wondered who it was, his name, his country of origin, but his identity was probably lost in the past, tea went back centuries. Closing his eyes to savour the next mouthful, he felt it invigorate his body in the same way water invigorated a man who had lasted forty-eight hours in the desert without.

Without the presence of his friend, he didn't stay long, little point, everyone else working there was a stranger to him. Finishing his tea, he walked up the High

Street, hearing the busker before seeing him. They exchanged their customary nods. After finishing his song, he asked Michael how things were.

"Had an unusual interview, wasn't like an interview but counted, if you understand what I mean."

"Not sure I follow, your expression indicates it was positive though," he replied laughing.

"Yeah, reckon so, I haven't received a job offer yet, but I believe my chances are good."

"Your luck's improving then."

"Yeah, how's yours today, have you been wowing the punters?"

"Actually, the town's quiet, people shopping on the Internet, a few years from now, and towns, as we recognise them will have disappeared."

"Some still like shopping in town."

"True, but they don't like the prices. What are you doing next?"

"Well, I've a couple more job adverts to check out."

"Keeping the momentum going, excellent idea, you seem on a good run."

"Yeah, it helps you stay positive about trying the next one. Better than getting knock backs."

"I know what you mean. Off you go then, wow somebody else."

"I'll do my best, see you around."

Michael walked away but was overwhelmed by another feeling of nausea. *Not again*! He went for a bench. Sitting down, the feeling intensified, and the ground started to swirl around him. He groaned and closed his eyes. All sense of reality disappeared.

Michael found himself back in the dirty, tiled tunnel amongst a mass of moving humanity.

The claustrophobic feeling of being penned, like the pigs and sheep in the town's cattle market, swept through his mind, raising a semblance of panic. What is this place? It was unlike anywhere he had seen, and he desperately wanted to leave, and quickly? Still, he couldn't move in any direction other than forward and he couldn't stop either. The pace was excruciatingly slow. Feet behind nipped the heels of his shoes, as his nipped the persons in front. The noise was deafening, human voices, almost indeterminable, like a swarm of bees, except for the voices closest to him, all complaining, all bothered by the conditions.

A rush of air swept down the tunnel lifting his fringe from his forehead; it wasn't fresh, laden with the stench of soot. The overweight man walked with a swagger, swinging one leg forward followed by the other in exaggerated fashion. His shoulders and head swayed side to side confidently, nobody would knock him off his feet. His sway allowed Michael a brief glimpse ahead before blocking it again.

The T-Junction was ominously closer, less than twenty yards, he could see the filthy white tiles disappearing left and right. Illuminated signs, to the side, shone a message; instructional or informational, he was unsure. Trying and failing to read the glowing letters, they blurred into orange blotches.

"Where the hell are we?" he called to nobody in particular.

"Hell is about right," somebody responded, laughing. "The same hell we endure every time we come here."

Michael glimpsed the distance to the junction as over-weight man swung his frame left. A few yards to go!

Two black arrows, just in front, pointed left and right. How intelligent, Michael thought sarcastically, since there was a tiled wall in front of him. He questioned the direction he should take, but wasn't convinced he had a choice. Reaching the junction, the pressure from behind forced him right. Then heads lowered in front, including over-weight man, and he saw clearly ahead. Steps, they were descending. Completely missing the first, he stumbled fully into over-weight man before regaining my balance in time for the second.

"Hey, watch it man," Over-weight man snapped, glancing behind him.

"Sorry, lost my footing."

"Well, be more careful."

Over the heads, he saw the swathe of humanity stretching into the distance. The area beyond the steps widened. How on earth would those descending fit into an already full space? They did, and he did, then after negotiating the final step he lost all sense of position as he was swallowed in the sea of bodies. People attempted to push past, and he was jostled forward, sideways and even backwards as those, more impatient, sought their destination. Finally, he stood still, not knowing where he should move to.

The images faded and his eyes opened. He was back on the bench outside the employment office block, no longer feeling nauseous, but healthy. Memories of his vision remained complete, and his experience still gripped him with fear. Why was this keep happening to him? Where was that place. Why did he keep going there? These questions, and more, required answers he could not access, adding to his insecurity and fear. He wished Mary was still at the Wimpy, but she finished her shift earlier.

Perhaps he should just go home. Checking his watch, it said nine am. It had happened again.

The weather had altered, a mixture of cloud and blue sky, a weakened sun blinking its presence in the gaps. The temperature was similar. A different day, different weather! So what day was it?

Michael stopped an elderly woman passing by."

"Sorry, what day is it, I've got my days muddled?"

"Don't worry love, happens to me regularly, but today is Tuesday and it's Tuesday all day."

"Thanks."

"Merry Christmas."

"Same to you."

Michael remained sitting, realising it wasn't just an evening or night lost, but a whole twenty-four hours. Why did this keep happening, was he sick, a mind problem?

"Oh God, it's dementia!"

Busking man walked by and gave him a nod.

"You're certainly up and about early, come by later and I'll play you a song. Anything you like."

Michael got up, smiled and walked with him to the High Street. It was so surreal. He was playing close by when Michael had felt sick and sat, now he was preparing for another day of busking. *What is this madness?*

They parted, and Michael decided to change the routine he had inadvertently created. After experiencing a vision, he followed it by seeking another job. Not today! Today he would go home and visit his sister, who he had not seen since her return. He would spend the day with her, the whole day, and tomorrow? Tomorrow, when he woke, he would work at the RSPCA.

Chapter 26:

The walk home was relaxingly uneventful. By the time Michael arrived he was feeling his normal self. Rarely home early mornings, he preferred this time to exercise, and pursue work. The house would be empty, apart from his sister. A dose of her, exactly what he needed to deter his mind from his troublesome worries. He wouldn't confide in her, as far as his visions were concerned, but anything else was open for discussion. She was refreshingly honest, direct, but not unkind.

For years when they were growing up, she assumed some of the responsibility of his care while their mother worked; undertaking the responsibilities without complaint, or viewing it as a burden. Michael loved her for the person she was. His father had given her an equally tough time, after she had left school, and she took all his perpetual, and sometimes harsh comments, without complaint. When she spoke back in response, he could never win a verbal confrontation with her, she was intelligent, clever and could defend herself with ease. Once he realised this, he backed down, avoiding confrontation whenever it seemed likely.

"You home, Rachel?" he called, waiting for her usual teasing reply.

"You better believe it Angel," she replied, appearing into the kitchen where he waited.

She moved quickly towards him and smothered him in her usual bearhug greeting. He laughed, having no reply to her physicality, not particularly wanting to prevent it. Like her mother, she often called him Angel too.

"Hello, baby brother, how's it going?"

"Sometimes good, sometimes not. How about you?"

"Same old, same old. Had a brilliant time, but glad to be home. Missed you, occasionally."

"Ditto," Michael smiled back.

"Just made tea, do you want one?"

"Yes, please."

"Coming up, and then you can explain the confrontation with dad."

"You heard?"

"Mum told me. She was worried about you, as was I when she told me what happened."

Michael remained quiet until she brought over the teas and sat beside him.

"So, what gives brother?"

"He got on my back once too often, and I fought back. Not the appropriate strategy you'd use, but it made him consider afterwards."

"Good for you. How are things between you now?"

Michael explained what happened before and after the football match.

"Wow, whatever you said, and however you said it, is irrelevant, it brought the response you needed."

"I'm not sorry for hitting back, but I'm ashamed at how I said it."

"Don't be, it's a reaction to a situation. He should have been far more encouraging with you. He had it coming."

"I guess so."

"So, what are you up to today?"

"Had an idea to spend quality time together. I've been feeling so negative recently and haven't made the effort I should have."

"Anything particular in mind?"

"I haven't considered that far; in truth, I'd be happy to do something different from job hunting."

"What about shopping?"

"No money."

"You got the job at the RSPCA."

"Yes, but it's monthly paid. And how do you know that?"

"I asked mum how you were doing, you know I like to keep an eye on you."

"I should have guessed."

"I can lend you some money if you need it?"

"Thanks, I appreciate that, but I want my independence. I'm sure Bruce at the RSPCA might advance me some of my pay before Christmas."

"Suit yourself, but the offer remains."

"Thanks. I'm happy to go shopping with you, though."

"Ok, I suggest we go to Cantry, have a meal out to make it more special and fun, better than Ashley."

"I seem to have lived in Ashley town lately with the job searching, so this is a good change."

An hour later they stepped off the bus in Cantry.

"Been thinking about you a bit lately."

"I should hope so, I'm your sister."

"I didn't mean generally. I was considering what you did when I was younger, taking care of me when mum worked."

"That's what older siblings do now and again."

"True, but they don't always do it like you?"

"What do you mean?"

"You never treated me like I was a burden, you took care of me properly and made our time together fun.

"That's a very mature perspective, but I appreciate you saying it, and know I love you too, soft boy."

Michael grinned, knowing his sister was deflecting. For all her intelligence and vocal skills, she was a big softie when you broke through her defence. Reaching her emotionally was easy for him; their understanding and trust in each other formed the core of their bond. She slipped her arm through his and changed the subject.

"So, what shall we buy the olds? You know we could get something together; I mean, from both of us, I'll cover it today and you can pay me back on payday. It will lessen the amount of our spending, which will help me; I'm not overly flushed with money, and your job probably isn't high paid. What do you reckon?"

"That sounds great, and really helpful Rachel, I appreciate it." Michael said, knowing for certain his sister was offering this purely for his benefit.

Michael explained about the other jobs he had applied for and shared the stories that accompanied them.

"You have a knack for being kind to others, brother, it's your gift you know, and the main reason mum and I call you Angel. I suppose you don't like being called that anymore?"

"When you and mum call me that, it doesn't bother me. At the risk of sounding a soft boy again, it's affectionate. I'm not keen for anyone else to call me Angel though."

Next, he told her about Mary and how she was very like her.

"I think that's why I like her so much. It's like being with a younger you."

"I'm not that flippin' old," Rachel said, with false indignance. "But that's sort of flattering, though. Do you like her as a girlfriend, or is she a potential girlfriend for the future?"

"I don't think so. At least, definitely not for the immediate future. I value her friendship. Many of my former mates lost female friends after dating them."

"Dating is an old-fashioned word, it's more normal these days to say you're seeing someone, or going out with someone. It's possible for friends to develop their relationship beyond just friends. And why not now?"

"Mum always uses dating as a word, so I guess that explains my use. Having her friendship is more important because I've lost most of my old ones."

"Mum told me about that. It's tough, but they don't deserve you as a friend if they can't stand by you when things are rough."

"Mary said that too."

"Sounds like you've made a good friend there. You should bring her round one day, I'd like to meet her."

"You going to check her out for me?"

"Don't need to. If she's good enough for you, she's good enough for me."

Michael smiled and changed the focus back to her.

"What about you? Any boyfriend on the scene? After all, you're not getting any younger?"

"Cheeky git," Rachel responded, laughing. "Sometimes I forget about that sharp wit of yours when we talk seriously."

"Couldn't resist it, you're so ripe for teasing sometimes. So, any boyfriend? I can't believe you haven't attracted any with your looks and personality."

"Aw, thanks Michael, but sadly no. I seem to attract the wrong type who look at me superficially and don't appreciate my other talents."

"What talents?"

"Oy, from compliments to teasing in two sentences, really?"

"What you really mean is they don't appreciate your intelligence, articulation and humanitarianism."

"Grief Michael, have you been planning to use the big vocabulary on me in advance."

"Actually, no! But those attributes sum you up and I reckon you'd be wasting your time with anyone who can't appreciate what you offer."

"Wow, you have really grown up a lot during the last couple of years."

"You're deflecting again."

She feigned innocence. "I don't know what you mean?"

"Every time I say something nice, you deflect, because behind those titles, you're a big softie."

Rachel stopped walking. "If anyone else said that, I would become defensive. But coming from you. Well, you couldn't say anything more complimentary. That you know me that well, at a deeper level of understanding, shows how much you care for me, brother, and I don't take what you offer for granted."

She hugged him fiercely, in the middle of the pavement, in front of the entire world. A show of affection normally only ever given in private. There were tears in her eyes when she told him she loved him.

The day passed wonderfully slowly. They shared fish and chips on a bench outside the city's cathedral, sorting the world's problems, and enjoying every second of each other's company. A perfect day; one which removed Michael temporarily away from his troubles. Later, that evening, Michael went to bed early feeling the onslaught of nausea again. When he woke, he was back on the bench outside the employment office. It had happened again!

Chapter 27:

Michael stopped an elderly woman passing by."

"Sorry, what day is it, I've got my days muddled?"

"Don't worry love, happens to me regularly, but today is Tuesday and it's Tuesday all day."

"Thanks."

"Merry Christmas."

"Same to you."

Michael muttered under his breath, *"unbelievable!"*

He rose and started walking towards the Wimpy, and Mary. Entering, he spotting her instantly, wiping the booth he liked to sit in. Sliding in, he smiled at her.

"You doing that just for me?" he smiled.

"I could wipe you down as well, you know."

"No need, I'm clean. Have loads to share with you, Mary."

"Good or bad, Michael?"

"Both, but it's happened again, the tunnel..."

Mary sensed his need to share.

"Wait here Michael, I'll get you a tea."

She rushed off quickly and returned in less than a minute with a steaming brew. She slid into the booth alongside him.

"Drink this Michael, relax and take your time," she said, moving closer and placing her hand on his.

"What's happening to me Mary, this is the third time I've had these visions, and on three different occasions I've lost time."

"It must be a loss of memory Michael, it's the only thing that makes sense."

"Did I see you yesterday, Mary."

"No, my day off, I have one off in the week because I work Saturdays."

"I should have been at the RSPCA, it's the third time I've missed a shift or forgotten one."

"Tell me about the vision."

"It was scary, the visions are awful, wherever this place is, it's horrible, and I feel panicked there. It's so real. Every time I wake, my hands smell sooty. Here, smell them yourself."

Mary laughed. "If I start smelling your hands in the café, I'll get some peculiar looks from the customers. But I believe you Michael."

Michael felt relief, hearing her words. She spoke the truth; he saw the compassion for his feelings in her face.

"Thanks, because I reckon, I'm losing my mind."

"Perhaps you're just tired, you've been on an emotional rollercoaster with the employment thing for ages. Perhaps your recent success is allowing the stress, you've been living with, escape, maybe it's coming out as these visions. Michael, I don't think it's with your mind. Mind problems often affect personalities and yours is fine."

"I'm glad for your friendship, Mary, because this weird stuff is freaking me out. There's nobody else to tell this to, who wouldn't laugh."

"You need to focus on something else. How many job adverts left to apply for?"

"There should be two in my wallet."

"Well, select one and let's examine it. This will give you the focus you need."

Michael retrieved one and lay it on the table.

Postal Service Requires
Fit and Able Persons
For the Delivery
Of Her Majesty's Mail.
Excellent Career Opportunities
Apply: The Ashley Sorting Office.

"Looks interesting," Mary said enthusiastically, "early starts and early finishes, plenty of the day left after your shift for other things.

"I've still got the sports centre job news to share with you and a day out with my sister."

"It can wait Michael. Let's get you moving again."

"I'm always up first, often out before anybody else rises and prepares for work. In truth, I feel better not seeing them prepare for work when I can't, so the early starts aren't a worry."

"What do you think, working for the Post Office?"

"There's a career opportunity, Mary, only the coaching job, has a career potential, so far."

"I think you should try this; it will clear your mind from your dreams or visions, and give you focus again."

"Ok, I'm on my way. Oh, and Mary."

"Yes?"

"Thanks for being here."

The Sorting Office was situated on an industrial estate to the north of town. Strange how these jobs had taken him in virtually every direction; It was half-an-hour's walk from the Wimpy. He'd visited several times before, collecting parcels for his parents, mostly Christmas presents from a variety of his relatives.

The route was simple but not exactly pleasant or aesthetically pleasing. Leaving town, you had to follow a busy A road until arriving at the Industrial Estate. Long, fairly straight, and with very narrow paths, it was dangerous in places where lorries thundered by so close and deafeningly. Many drivers failed to adhere to the speed limit, taking advantage of the straight nature of it.

The scenery was mundane too. On both sides, tall and thick hedgerows grew wildly, blocking the potential view of the countryside beyond. The estate was situated a mile down the road.

Reaching the A-road, he hugged the inside of the path as he walked. There were two narrower sections, where lorries or busses coming in opposite directions couldn't pass without mounting the kerb. The spots were marked with speed restrictions, clearly signed, but it didn't appear too many drivers paid attention to them. He was glad when he turned onto the estate, leaving the noisy road behind.

Michael had always enjoyed looking at new cars on a showroom forecourt, and the first business held a huge plot housing the biggest car retailer in town. A Ford dealership. Every car in the showroom was a new Ford, while those on the forecourt were a variety of makes, mostly second hand, and taken in part exchange for a new vehicle. He wanted a car, like the one his brother bought last year. He was first in the family to own one, after his father, and was proud of that fact.

The plot next door, was leased by an agricultural dealership and contained a range of machines on display; tractors, ploughs, even a combine harvester sat on the forecourt.

Next to that, a company specialising in storage followed by the sorting office, with the familiar red paint adorning the post boxes in town.

Chapter 28:

A sign guided visitors along a narrow path at the side of the building, leading to the customer service door. Inside a cold, and empty space served as a collection area.

One wall contained a window with an enclosed counter on the opposite side, filthy dirty, not exactly sharing a welcome. A bell on the wall accompanied a simple sign saying: Please Ring for Service. He rang it, hearing it sound in the vastness of the sorting room, hidden beyond the counter. A few seconds later, a sour faced youth appeared at the desk.

"What can I do for you, mate?"

"I've come to see somebody about the job adverts," Michael told him.

"Interviews are by appointment only," he said coldly.

"I wasn't expecting an interview, just somebody who can explain the job details."

"What's to tell, you collect mail and deliver it," he said simply.

"Must be more to it, who can I speak to?"

"I'll see if my supervisor is free."

Disappearing before Michael could thank him, a feeling the youth couldn't be bothered washed over him. Minutes passed before a man came to the glass window.

He said good morning, passed him a booklet and an application form.

"The booklet reveals the job requirements and contains application form instructions, any questions should be answered in there. If you require a tour of the operations room, and a more detailed explanation, an appointment with my manager is necessary. That's problematic at the moment, he's off sick. No one else is available. All applicants, successfully gaining interviews, receive a tour of the facilities as a matter of course, so perhaps the best way forward is to fill the form before you leave. Do you have a pen? Alternatively, you can apply on-line at home."

Michael felt disappointed when the man left; all week he'd met friendly people, happy to share their time and talk, here, he gained the impression they couldn't be bothered. He sat down and began filling in the form. Half completed, the door opened and an elderly woman, heavily hunched, entered and approached the counter. Too short to reach the bell, Michael rose and rang it for her.

"Thank you, young man!" she said, flashing a half smile. "They didn't think about those vertically challenged when they installed this," she said ruefully, then smiled.

He smiled back but didn't answer. The bell was not positioned particularly high; but she was incredibly short. He returned to his application form, but noticed the second appearance of the sour faced youth. The woman handed him her collection form, and he stated *two-minutes* before disappearing. Michael finished his form and stood behind her, ready to hand it in when the youth returned. He didn't wait long, he returned quicker than expected, placing a jiffy bag and a larger parcel on the counter, before lifting the glass panel so the woman could take them.

"Sign here, luv," he ordered, pushing a small pad towards her and giving her a pen. She duly signed.

"I don't think I could carry the parcel back to town dear," she said disappointedly.

"I'm going back to town in a minute, I would be happy to help you if you like," Michael offered.

"Oh, thank you so much, how thoughtful," she said, sharing a fuller smile than her previous attempt.

"That's sorted then," the youth said.

Michael passed his completed application form over, and he disappeared from view. He picked up the parcel. It was large enough to be awkward and was fairly heavy, too.

"I'm afraid I don't walk fast, young man, short legs you see," she told me.

"That's alright; I'm not in a rush, we can take our time."

She was right, the pace was painfully slow, so slow, he felt he was moving in slow motion; Neil Armstrong walking on the moon surface.

"They're going to lock me up!" she said, breaking the silence that evolved while they concentrated on the walk.

"Pardon me?"

"They're going to lock me up," she repeated.

"Who is, and where?" he asked.

"My son and his lazy wife, they're putting me into a home."

"Why?"

"They say I can't care for myself properly, I'm too old and accident prone."

"What's your thoughts about that?" Michael asked, not sure how to respond to her revelation.

"My house is clean and tidy, I cook twice a day, but I forget things, more than before."

Michael started recalling the time he had lost recently, simply removed from his conscious memory, and understood exactly how frustrating it was for him, probably her too.

"I forget things, especially if they don't seem very important," Michael told her, attempting to make her feel better than she obviously did.

"That's what I said; everybody forgets occasionally, but they say I forget everything. I do all I'm supposed to, I have a rota for each day, it covers housework, shopping, paying bills and makes sure I get enough exercise. Even my meals are on it. Oh, and I have a budget for my spending. I'm probably more organised than the queen, she has people taking care of everything."

"Would you like that?"

"Not on your Nelly, I enjoy organising for myself and I value privacy."

"Sounds like me, I enjoy doing things for myself too."

"Fifty years I've lived in my house, raised a son, outlived my brothers, and my husband, and I've coped so far. Now, because I'm old, they want me in a home. I think it's so they don't have to worry about me, I bet their monthly visits would stop too."

"I'm sure they don't think that, but when my grandfather was old, before he died, my parents worried."

"Bet they didn't put him in a home though did they."

Michael didn't answer; they hadn't, but he knew his mother visited daily, ensuring he was well cared for.

The year he died, they had cancelled their holiday, because she was worried about his health.

They fell silent, and Michael considered life from her perspective, which wasn't easy. He couldn't imagine being as old as her. Having a fit, healthy mind but without a fit and healthy body. It must be hard, their walk to town was evidence enough, already taken twice as long returning as he took getting there. He wondered how it felt outliving your family, seeing them die, until only her son remained. How many friends did the woman have? Did she see them regularly? Did she have visitors apart from the monthly visit from her son?

The more he considered it, getting old was not a good prospect. His mother always said, as her children grew up, they became a constant reminder she was getting old. She never seemed old to him, and he never noticed the changes in her, unless old photographs reminded him of the family at earlier stages in their lives. She always appeared fit and healthy, his father too, but was life becoming more difficult for them as they aged?

Chapter 29

Closing in on the town, they finally left the A-road. Michael was relieved, the parcel seemed heavier now. She complimented his manners as he insisted on her walking on the inside of the path. My husband made me do that, she explained; Michael replied his father made his mother do the same. The topic of conversation had altered minutes ago. She asked him about school and job hunting, and he shared the unlikely accounts of his interviews.

"You'll get a job if you conduct yourself in the manner you have," she said warmly. "You're polite, helpful with great manners; that impresses most; they won't forget you," she encouraged.

Then she asked if they could stop at a bench and rest. Funny, he thought, he seemed to sit on benches all the time recently.

"Would you like a cup of tea?" she asked.

The elderly had an infinity with cups of tea, his parents, not exceptionally old, and grandparents always had a pot of tea made. Lately, he had an infinity with it too.

"I would love to join you for one."

"That would be lovely, dear; I can't remember the last time I shared tea with a friend. There's a little cafe near the church called, The Old Cottage Tearooms, I haven't been there for ages but they make an amazing cup of Earl Grey, you ever tried Earl Grey dear?"

"I haven't, but there's a first time for everything," Michael stated, altering the direction they walked.

The tea rooms were quaint, old-fashioned. A waitress, dressed in black with a white pinafore apron, led them to a table and gave them a menu.

"They bake lovely scones with cream and jam and with a pot of tea. It's called a Kentish Tea."

His mouth watered at her description; he hadn't realised he was hungry.

"How about a pot of Earl Grey between us and a scone each?" she suggested smiling, "perhaps you would order, my husband always ordered for me. He took such care of me."

The waitress returned and Michael placed the order.

"My generation prefers a man ordering, perhaps not nowadays, as young women want their equal rights, but once the men always ordered."

Michael was happy to please her, she reminded him of his own grandmother.

"We've been chatting almost an hour and we haven't introduced ourselves?"

He realised she was right.

"I said I forget things sometimes, and I clearly forgot that," Michael told her, grinning. "I'm Michael, Michael Ferguson."

"I'm Lucy, Lucy Bourne."

She held out a frail, wrinkly hand for him to shake, and he took it gently. They both laughed. The scone and tea arrived, and he thanked the waitress who poured them both a cup. He sipped the brew and discovered he liked the aromatic flavour.

“This is good, an unusual flavour. Do you know what?”

“It’s blended with Bergamot; it makes it so good. My mother used to make a Bergamot infusion when she was alive; I loved the flavour of it. Many old skills are lost these days, as manufacturers make everything for you. Try your scone, I promise you’ll love that too.”

She was right, the scone was huge, and the pots of jam and cream accompanying it were equally generous. There was no more discussion until they had devoured them and licked their lips in appreciation. Michael finished pouring a second cup, when a member of the clergy entered the tea room, stopping in surprise at seeing Lucy.

“Lucy, lovely to see you, how are you?”

“Reverend Green, lovely to see you, too. I’m fine, much better, especially after eating one of the finest scones I’ve ever tasted. Allow me to introduce you to Michael Ferguson, a friend and saviour of mine.”

He laughed at her description and shook hands with the Michael.

“Would you care to join us Reverend, there’s enough tea left in this pot?”

“That’s very kind, and I accept your offer, Michael.”

He carried a chair from an adjacent table and sat down.

“So how are you really Lucy, health-wise I mean?”

“I’m better, the pneumonia has cleared and I’m my old self again, although a little slow. I get out of breath easily”

“That’s great news, but the breathing is to be expected. God takes care of his own, for sure.”

Michael called the waitress, seeking another cup for the Reverend, and pouring when it came. He stayed out of the conversation, allowing them catch up before Lucy explained how they met at the sorting office, and how he had carried her parcel. He commented on Michael's thoughtfulness, suggesting good deeds often led to new friendships.

The Reverend's conversation altered course as he enquired about Lucy's son. Michael noticed the smile, constant for the last ten minutes, drop as she informed him her son wanted to place her into a home. He, as Michael had, asked her how she felt, and she answered with an identical reply.

"Maybe you are viewing this the wrong way, Lucy. You said your son is worried you can't care for yourself. That's not true, but there are other important things needed in life?" Michael asked suddenly, as a thought crossed his mind.

"What do you mean?" she asked.

"I'm talking about friendship and companionship. Looking after your physical needs, you cope with, but getting out and about is problematic, especially after your illness. You said you'd outlived your family and most of your friends. perhaps you need a new family and new friends. You can get that in a home."

"The boy is astute, Lucy; you've been alone for years; I know you don't have the contact with others you really need. You're the most sociable person I've ever met, you enjoy caring for, and helping people, to the point where you forget your own needs. It isn't selfish, doing what Michael suggests, because by taking care of yourself you'd become stronger and be more capable of caring for others. In a home, most living there belong to your age group, you'll be able to care for them, and make friends easily. Your social life will be as full as you allow it to be."

"I hadn't considered that, but I don't want anybody cleaning for me and taking away my independence."

"They do that, only if you can't. Most care homes allow you to be as independent as possible. I visited some of my elderly congregation at a home last week and they were clearly happy and content. If you like, we could visit one together."

"If I went, just to check it out you understand, would you join me Michael, I'd value your opinion and thoughts about it."

Michael was surprised, but responded positively.

"I'd be pleased to, Lucy," he responded, and she smiled delightedly.

"When would you like to go?"

"Now! Strike whilst the iron is hot, as they say."

"Do I assume you're thinking positively about this? Choosing to go into a home yourself, means it becomes your decision, not your son's, and you choose the home you like," the Reverend added.

"Where's the home you mentioned, Reverend?"

"Don't worry Michael, I've a car outside. I'd be pleased to drive there and introduce the staff and my residential friends."

Lucy raised her hand to get the waitresses attention and asked for the bill. She brought it, folded, on a small, decorative, chrome tray. Lucy reached into her bag for her purse, but the reverend stopped her.

"Tea is on me today, Lucy," he said strongly, suggesting he wanted no argument.

He paid, and they left.

The residential home was situated at the outskirts of town. Michael was surprised to discover it was one of the large buildings he passed walking to the cemetery. As residential homes went, it was not exceptionally large, but cosy. After the Reverend revealed its location, he told Lucy about Jennifer and her new studio at the cemetery gatehouse.

"I used to paint in the past," she said enthusiastically, promising to pay Jennifer a visit once the studio was in use.

She rang the bell herself, and a woman in a light blue uniform opened the door.

"Hello, I've come to view the accommodation here," Lucy said, taking charge of the situation. Reverend Green winked at Michael as they were shown in. The woman asked Michael if he was Lucy's grandson.

"I'd be proud to have a fine young man like him for a grandson, but alas he's not," Lucy answered for him.

During the tour, the Reverend and Michael dropped back a little.

"She's got the bit between her teeth; better if we stay in the background, allow her to decide things for herself. By the way, you were considerate toward her earlier. She can care of herself, adequately, but she lacks purpose and people in her life. This place is perfect, but she must decide that herself."

The visit stretched for an hour before they left with the offer of the Reverend running them home. Michael asked to be dropped in town. Lucy was positively glowing; the enthusiasm she showed, toward the residential home, suggested she wanted to move there. Michael felt pleased for her and strangely sad as the Reverend pulled into a layby, close to the town centre, for him.

"Thank you for your help, Michael. And for the kindness and consideration you gave me today. I'm definitely moving in there, and I'd love it if you visited."

He promised he would, and she asked him to pass her the parcel he had carried. Giving it to her, she carefully peeled off the stamps.

"I'm guessing somebody in your family collects stamps, probably your dad, and these have come all the way from Brazil," she said, passing them across.

He thanked her and asked her how she knew.

"Always someone in a family collecting them," she said, as he tucked them into his pocket.

He said goodbye to the Reverend and moved away from the car, waving as it sped off towards Lucy's home.

Chapter 30:

Walking leisurely back to the High Street, Michael had almost forgotten the events of earlier. He stopped at the first available bench, intending to read the last advert. Unexpectedly, it was one bench he had not used recently, and he remembered why the thought of sitting on so many amused him. As a younger boy, his sister enjoyed taking him into town when meeting her friends. A few brought their younger siblings too, enjoying the responsibility of caring for them, and pretending to be adults.

She was amused by his insistence on sitting on every bench he passed; his efforts encouraged the others siblings to follow suit. Throughout his young life they played a game they christened Bench Sit; he remembered the way they counted them and his recall suggested fourteen was the record for any one visit. He smiled at the memory; his sister was always particularly good to him and his gentle nature and infinite patience modelled hers. Everybody loved her, for the person she was.

He suddenly realised he hadn't received stickers from the sorting office, feeling disappointed his success at collecting them had not continued. Technically, he had not been interviewed, though. Only four more required to fill his card. Pulling it from his shirt pocket, the stamps

Lucy gave him followed, falling to the ground. He reached down for them, noticing each stamp had words printed on them. He guessed in Spanish, but couldn't read them, or recognise the buildings in the images on them.

He turned them to check they were not marked, and on the reverse side, were two stickers he believed he missed out on. Peeling them off, he noticed the letters N and L and he carefully applied them to his card. *Two to go and one final advert to try for,* he mused, placing it into his pocket.

The sun emerged from behind cotton wool clouds. He hadn't noticed its temporary retreat but felt the full force of its radiance, making him squint and narrow his eyes to slits. Tendrils of heat followed the brightness permeating his shirt, invigorating his skin, and encouraging him to take pleasure in its embrace. He closed his eyes, enhancing the sensation of its touch.

He was back in the tunnel. Over-weight man swaggered in front; the mass of humanity consuming all. There was no fear this time; a morbid sense of familiarity coursed through, as he was swept along the tunnel by those around him. He waited calmly for the T junction to appear. Still, he failed to read the orange messages on the electronic information boards, but that didn't concern him either.

The T junction appeared and he was forced to the right; the stairs followed, descending towards another mass of humanity. He failed to prevent himself from missing the first step and stumbled into over-weight man; the events unfolding as before. He heard the same words too.

"Hey, watch it, man." He answered identically before reaching the bottom step and becoming consumed in the sea of bodies.

The push from behind remained relentless, as increasing numbers descended the steps, but from this point, everything was new. The forward momentum slowed as people ahead reached their destination and ceased moving. He was penned in by the crush of humanity, like a bunch of grapes, grown so tightly together, that cutting a portion was impossible. Finally, his movement ceased too. Body pushed against body. No personal space respected, becoming tighter by the second as more descended, cramming in behind. Turning his head side to side, the rest of his body totally restricted, he discerned nothing but heads everywhere, completely concealed his destination.

While waiting, a rush of wind bathed the humanity. The same soot-laden wind smelt and felt before, only stronger. Following this, a sound increasing as it drew nearer, a whining sound, growing to deafening proportions, drowning the buzzing of voices around him. It ceased suddenly, and those in front shuffled forward again.

Whatever the sound was, his distance from it, remained a mystery, but he was carried relentlessly closer. His heart beat faster. A sudden hiss and the whining sound evolved again. Those in front ceased moving. He ceased moving, forced to remain in his position, incapable of moving in any direction. Still, his whereabouts eluded him, as did the reason for his presence. He decided to ask somebody.

The image faded and Michael's eyes opened. He sat on a bench outside the employment office block. The sun wallowed low in the sky and the air was fresher than inside the tunnel. A significant lack of life in town was noticeable. Checking his watch, it was nine o'clock, and he realised he had lost time again. He needed the day. He asked an old woman passing by. She looked familiar.

"Sorry love, but what day of the week is it, I seem to have got my days muddled?" Michael asked.

"Don't worry love, I do that all the time, but today is Tuesday, and it's Tuesday all day."

"Thanks."

"Merry Christmas."

"Same to you."

Always Tuesday, always Tuesday, he mused.

Laughing at the absurdity of his situation, he pulled the card from his shirt pocket and checked the stickers inside. There were still nine, with two vacant spaces for those uncollected. He returned it, not planning to waste time trying to explain the unexplainable. He still believed it advisable not to discuss this with anybody but Mary. What would they think of it; probably, he was spinning a yarn, or maybe he was losing his grip on reality?

He wished he could discover his vision's location. Not recognising it, bothered him, almost as much as the increasing regularity of them. Perhaps he could test his sister on this, pretend it was a game, and she had to guess the place he described. Yes, that might work. If she couldn't guess the location, then maybe his brother, he was well- travelled, and he might recognise it. Devious really, but it might get him answers.

Then the disappointment of the Post Office job. He had achieved little there; and he was not optimistic of getting an interview. Pity, prior to that, everything was positive. Helping Lucy was pretty cool, even in a small way; she was a kind person, deserving the help anyone gave her.

Chapter 31:

Michael decided to follow his normal procedure after receiving a vision. Walk to the Wimpy and discuss it with Mary. He hoped today was not her day off; everything about her shifts seem to differ after he lost time. He passed the busker, half way through a blues number, the music sounded cool. Pity, listening was out of the question, his visit to Mary was more important. He gave him a nod, as usual, and received one back, but carried on walking. She spotted him approaching through the window before he saw her.

"I've only just started my shift; We have a shortage of staff this week so I'm working two half days instead of having a day off. I finish at twelve. I wanted to ask you over to my Grans for dinner on Sunday. You can walk Charlie with me if you like."

"Thanks Mary, I'd like that a lot," smiling at the breathless manner in which she spoke.

"I have to work now, but if you return at twelve, perhaps you'd walk me home."

"Sounds like a plan."

Mary disappeared into the kitchen area, and Michael walked back towards the busker, with more than two hours to wait before returning for Mary. Two hours was excessive for listening to music, he should have stayed for a tea before leaving, too late now. Reaching the busker, he had stopped playing and was sitting on a bench.

"Back again, young man?"

"Have a couple of hours to pass before meeting my friend."

"It's a little cold to spend it listening to me, if that's what you intended."

"No, perhaps half an hour, I went Christmas shopping with my sister and we struggled to find a gift for my brother. Thought I'd have another look."

"Christmas is a great time if families get together."

"We always do, have our routines and rituals I suppose, but it works for us. What about you?"

"I'll be spending it with my wife, love of my life that one."

"How long have you been together?"

"Seems like forever, couldn't imagine any life without her."

"It's good that you still feel that way."

"I hope you find someone to make you happy like she does me."

"Plenty of years for that, my focus is on work, it's my priority."

"And is the search still positive?"

"Had a setback at the Post Office."

"What happened?"

"Not sure, the people I spoke to didn't seem interested."

"All sorts of folk in the world, most with issues taking their attention."

"That's how it seemed."

"No worries then, it wasn't you, probably something else. Have you any more interviews lined up?"

"One final job to investigate. Haven't looked at it yet. I've been sharing the process with my friend. She has all sorts of advice and techniques I wouldn't have considered. She's helped a lot, so far."

"Great to have a good friend."

They continued talking, sharing thoughts about a variety of issues, and soon passed the time Michael allowed for listening to the man's singing.

"I should get going," Michael announced.

"And I should start singing. Won't earn much today if I don't. Good chatting to you, lad."

"Likewise," Michael answered, smiling as he turned away.

Michael passed the remaining time searching for a present for his brother, before walking back to the Wimpy.

It was busy inside and Michael saw the reduced staff struggling to manage the volume of customers. By his calculation, Mary should have finished five minutes ago, but was displaying no signs of finishing her shift. He wondered if she'd been asked to stay on. He slipped into that last remaining empty booth and waited for her to spot him. Ten minutes passed before she did.

"Sorry Michael, I've volunteered another hour, we're so busy; the rest of the girls wouldn't be able to cope alone."

"I guessed as much, but I've had enough killing time outside now. It's cold out there. If I order a tea, I'll wait here until you finish."

"Sorry Michael, I had no way of warning you. You haven't shared your phone number yet."

"You're right, we'll do that first when you finish, but don't apologise, Mary, stuff happens sometimes."

"Thank you. I'll get you a tea."

Michael ended up having two teas before Mary finished. She walked by to tell him before disappearing to retrieve her bag and coat. Outside, she invited him to share.

"Come on, tell me about the Post Office job as we walk."

"Little to share, Mary, didn't go well. I had an excellent time with a lady called Lucy, then another vision."

"Oh no, not another one. You don't seem too phased this time. You were scared before, why the change?"

"No idea, it felt completely different, even though I travelled further. I heard weird noises, felt sooty wind, and still the location is unknown. Bizarrely, despite being extended, it seemed familiar and there was comfort in that."

"It's like a TV series, except everything gets repeated before being extended."

"Yes, it is like that."

Michael described the extended part for her, but she refrained from commenting, and he assumed she had no explanation or thoughts yet.

"You've one more job to try for, when are you going for it. She asked, changing the subject.

"As soon as possible, perhaps after, things will become normal again. Do you realise, I've missed all my shifts at the RSPCA this week? I'll be surprised if the job's still mine."

"It's possible you did the shifts, but don't remember them."

"I hope you're right, Mary." But Michael was unconvinced.

"Let's examine the last job, then.

Chapter 32:

Michael retrieved his wallet and removed the last advert just as they reached a bench in the park.

"Here it is Mary."

Give Birth to a New and Exciting Career.
Travel all over the Country
with the Rail Network.
Recruiting Now.
Apply M. Stratton
Derrybrook Station
London.

"It's good money working on the trains, and the career prospects are excellent," she said positively.

He read it again, nodding his affirmation.

This was different. His father had suggested working for the railways, but had spoken about engineering, and although he didn't mind getting his hands dirty, the work had not appealed to him. The idea of engineering had cooled any thoughts of working for the railways, and he hadn't considered other careers within it. He wondered what field this job was in, the advert didn't say.

"It won't take a lot of effort to research it, Mary. I could get answers at the local station."

"When will you go?"

"I'll walk there first thing tomorrow. Now I need a change in routine, and the company of a good friend. It might be cold, but it's a good day for walking."

"Sound's good, anywhere special in mind?"

"Somewhere quiet, out in the countryside, perhaps."

"That's easy to arrange, it starts at the end of my road. We could collect Charlie too."

Reaching Mary's house, they soon discovered that her grandmother and Charlie were not home. Mary made a flask of tea for their walk and left a note explaining where she was.

As they walked the rest of her road, it narrowed, no more than a lane, and clearly unused, judging by the autumnal debris still littered on it. The change was abrupt, from town to countryside in a few steps. Not only the scenery changed. Sounds from traffic were immediately left behind to be replaced with winter birdsong.

"Wow, it's so peaceful here."

"I love bringing Charlie along here, I can let him off the lead, he loves it."

"Dogs always get more exercise if they're off the lead. You're so lucky to have all this next door."

"It's more Michael, I come here to think, when I'm happy or lonely. It seems to suit every type of mood."

"I can understand that. Perhaps, if it's ok, we can talk more about my visions."

"They're still bothering you, despite not fearing them so much. I still believe you should share these with a professional."

"Maybe in the future, but I need answers first."

"What questions do you want answers to?"

"The key question is, where is it leading me to? What's the point to all of this, where am I going? Each time I experience a vision it takes me further. A little like reading a book; page by page, the story unravels. I don't have a good feeling about the ending."

"What do you mean?"

"I haven't anything concrete to base that on except that if it's a happy conclusion, why draw it out? It makes more sense to assume it's the opposite."

"I disagree Michael. I dream a lot, more happy dreams than unhappy. And while they've never followed a pattern like yours, they take equal amounts of time. The details I remember, good or bad, are similar in quantity."

"So, you reckon I'm thinking wrong?"

"I didn't say that exactly, but you might be. What if your dream is based on a story, you've either read or watched? It's possible. I've started watching films and fallen asleep before the ending. A story without an end is so much less memorable. Same with books. You start a book, don't enjoy it, and stop reading it after a couple of chapters, sometimes even less."

"You have a knack of making everything sound sensible, Mary. Honestly, though, do you think I have a mental problem?"

"You don't behave like someone with a mental problem, Michael. I don't believe your inventing what you see deliberately either, so for now it's just a mystery. Do you think you have a mental problem?"

"No, everything seems normal, the way I speak, act, and think. Everything except these visions. I've woken, on a bench, outside the employment office so many times now and lost days without a reasonable explanation. If I told anybody else, apart from you, they'd think I was going mad."

"You're not going mad; you don't act mad at all."

Mary slipped an arm through his.

"You don't mind if I link arms with you?"

"Of course not. My sister does the same when we're out together."

"I'm glad Michael, I really like our relationship. It's safe, no expectations, no judging and no pressure. I'm thinking you're probably the best friend I've ever had."

"That makes two of us then," Michael, responded, smiling.

"I've got to go back soon, help Gran with some housework. She struggles with the hoover. You can come back, stay for a bite to eat."

"Normally, I'd say yes to food in a heartbeat, but I'm feeling tired today and I want to be up early to visit the railway station. I'm really curious about the job on offer."

"Fair enough, but you'll still come for Sunday dinner, though?"

"Wouldn't miss it for the world."

They walked back to her house and Michael started home. Already the day was fading as the light lost its intensity. Despite this, he lingered in the town centre, window shopping for the second time for his brother, and frustrated by the lack of inspiration. The busker was still playing and Michael took a seat nearby to listen. The next thing Michael noticed was waking up on the bench outside the employment office block. It had happened again, the second time without a vision.

Checking his watch, it was nine o'clock, and he realised time had been lost again. He needed the day. He asked an old woman passing by. She looked familiar.

"Sorry love, but what day of the week is it, I seem to have got my days muddled?" Michael asked.

"Don't worry love, I do that all the time, but today is Tuesday, and it's Tuesday all day."

"Thanks."

"Merry Christmas."

"Same to you.

Chapter 33:

Same time and day. Why was it he could not progress from Tuesday? A shift at the RSPCA seemed further away than ever. Losing time was happening at an increasing rate too, as many times without visions as with. He decided immediately. The station and the job. He rose, leaving the bench behind, and started walking.

The route was identical to the one leading to the sports centre. The station was further along Station Avenue. Confirming mentally this was his best course of action, he head in that direction.

He walked at a brisk pace, trying to take his mind from the haunting images which, while not reappearing in vision format this time, still installed an ominous feeling of dread. He focussed on Mary, in particular on how helpful and considerate she was. It worked and soon it altered towards the job and a multitude of questions that centred on the position he sought. From a young age he liked the railway station, it remained old worldly, not yet modernised and brought in line with the present. Taking the train was how his father travelled for years before buying a car, and he still considered their journeys together, as a small child, a treat.

The old wooden bridge, painted numerous times, still spanned the railway lines, and remained the only way to access the opposite platform. Twenty-two steps up and twenty-two steps down. Michael always enjoyed standing at the middle of the bridge as a train passed by, laughing when enveloped in the diesel smoke. That seemed a lifetime ago. The trains ran cleaner these days. Many a time he had begged his father to wait with him until the train they had embarked from left the station, so it would pass underneath him. He always waited alongside him; even now, when travelling together by train, instead of the car, to the south coast to visit relatives, he asked Michael if he wanted to pause on the bridge. These days he refused, too mature now, but the memory always raised a smile.

Crossing the bridge to the ticket office, it was the only place to meet a member of the Rail Service. Small stations like Ashley being manned fully had long passed. He couldn't remember the previous time he witnessed two or more members of staff there. The small platform cafe, had closed too. Once it served commuters travelling to London, but the trade no longer sustained it.

The station required painting and the old red, wooden benches had been replaced with metal equivalents; cold looking benches, offering nothing toward maintaining the character of the platform. Moving to the ticket office, he was pleased to see the absence of a queue, the rush hour finishing an hour ago. The man behind the glass fronted booth greeted him with a hearty *morning* and asked where he was travelling to. Michael explained he sought information about the jobs the Rail Service were advertising.

"They're advertising for ticket collectors and stewards for the long-haul trains. That interest you?" he asked in a friendly manner.

"The stewarding sounds interesting, especially if it means I travel all over the country," Michael responded.

"That's guaranteed. I travelled for twenty-two years before changing for the sedate pace of station life."

"The advert says I need to apply at Derrybrook, where exactly is that? I've never heard of it."

"A small station, outside the heart of London, but close enough to smell it," he replied, and Michael did not exactly understand his comment.

Michael had never visited London by train; he had visited London less than most, and only to football grounds like Wembley. They travelled by car then, and visiting the city properly had never been an option.

"Who's conducting the job interviews?"

Michael pulled out his wallet removing the advert.

"M. Stratton, the advert says, no idea if a man or a woman."

"It's a woman, Muriel, is her name, lovely lady and in the family way, so I'm told. She'll be a great mum that one, patience of a saint."

Michael thought it sounded promising until he enquired about the price of a return ticket and breathed in deeply as a response. The man noticed his discomfort and smiled.

"Don't worry, if you're applying for the job, the travel is free."

Michael inhaled a breath of relief.

"Right then, I'll have a return ticket to Derrybrook please."

"Good for you, good luck with the interview."

"I don't have an interview, I'm trying to be proactive, meet the right people before they decide who to interview; trying to make an impression."

"Sounds like a sensible tactic. There's always a huge list of applicants. Make sure, if you see Muriel, you tell her Bert in Ashley wishes her well and hopes everything is easy with the pregnancy. Train comes in seven minutes if it's on time."

Michael promised to relay his message and walked further onto the platform. He stood near the edge looking down the track, as he had done many times in the past, liking to see the signal change; waiting for the tiny speck in the distance to grow into the full size of the train as it arrived, and listening to the track sing as it got closer.

Litter collected down the track, masses of it, of all different types, spoiling the scene. It was a shame the railways didn't employ people to collect it and cut back the weeds.

The tracks, in Michael's opinion, were special. They promised a journey, a route to new and exciting, or quaint and relaxing destinations. The promise of a surprise guaranteed, would be more attractive if you viewed clean, uncluttered tracks.

Not renowned for punctuality; there were many complaints of trains arriving consistently late, making the commuters subsequently late for work. He had witnessed complainers on television, and listened to the multitude of excuses from the Rail Service. Funny how they only interviewed people, unhappy with the service. Michael wouldn't complain, he loved riding the trains.

He witnessed the train's imminent arrival long before it reached the station, waiting patiently as it slowed and came to a halt. Pressing the button to open the carriage door, it hesitated before responding, but closed quickly after he boarded. He decided he liked the loud sound it made as it locked firmly, securing him safely, as he walked down the carriage.

Chapter 34:

Unlike most carriages, this one was deserted, and his choice of where to sit limitless. Years ago, once the train was underway, he could lift seat cushions, checking for small change fallen from pockets. Something his father had shown him when he was small. Always a thrill for a child finding coins under them. Michael's grandfather taught his father when he was young. It seemed natural to pass the task onto Michael. Now that was impossible, the cushions were fixed, but he smiled at the memory.

For a moment, he sat, waiting for the journey to start. London! A tingle of excitement stirred his senses. As soon as the train left the station he focused on the scenes outside, passing at break neck speed.

This was a slow train, stopping at every station between here and Derrybrook. According to the map above the carriage entrance, there were twenty stops on route and this train would stop at all of them. He guessed the journey would last more than an hour to complete, but he wasn't bothered and he wasn't in any rush.

The train slowed while passing through villages and towns, speeding up through the countryside. The fields, overgrown with wheat a few months ago, were greyish-brown, and recently ploughed. He saw several tractors pulling disc-harrows behind, breaking up the clods of earth the ploughs had turned. Some fields held a semblance of green, winter vegetables stoically withstood the cold of this time of year.

Greener fields of grass held fattening sheep or dairy cows and, seeing them, he remembered Ashley Market where his mother took him to visit to watch the auctions. The most amazing pleasure about a train journey was that you viewed everything in such a short period. Positioned so much higher, than in a car, meant you viewed beyond the hedgerows and deep into the heart of the countryside.

The train slowed, approaching another stop, and he watched to see who boarded, strangely nobody did, in fact the station appeared empty and the train pulled away without increasing its load.

The door between carriages slid open and a pleasant-looking woman with golden coloured hair appeared and slid it shut behind her. She was dressed in the same Rail Service uniform that all their personnel wore, dark slacks and jacket with a white shirt. The jacket was open and he noticed the woman was heavily pregnant. The buttons on the shirt threatened to burst their restraints at any moment. She shuffled, or was it waddled, towards him and then greeted him with a cheery hello. He reached into his pocket for his wallet, where he had stowed away his ticket, and retrieved it ready for offering.

"Not many on this train today. You have the whole carriage to yourself. It's not a scheduled train; we are just moving carriages up the line for use in the city," she informed.

"I thought it was quiet, for this early in the day," Michael responded in a friendly way.

He passed her his ticket before she asked for it and watched as she clipped it with a tool similar to a pair of pliers. She returned it, and he noticed the shaped nick she had cut from it.

"Off to Derrybrook then?" she commented having read the destination on his ticket.

"Yes, somebody to see about a job," he told her enthusiastically.

"Good luck with that," she said, and he thanked her.

Then she groaned out loud, her face turning s white Michael thought she would pass out. Jumping up, he helped lower her into his now vacant seat.

"Are you ok?" he asked, instantly regretting the question, since it was perfectly clear she was in pain.

"Sorry, I've been getting false alarms all week that the baby is coming. The pain takes your breath away and then feelings of nausea, you get the idea. It's not actually due for a couple of weeks and I've only the coming weekend left at work before maternity leave."

She took a sharp intake of breath as another pain racked her body and then started panting rhythmically. He wasn't alarmed about that, knowing mum's to be were trained to breathe in certain ways to ease the pain. She closed her eyes, trying to control both, and he waited for her to relax before speaking again.

"Can I help in any way?" he asked.

"That's sweet, but this is what we women have to endure in order to receive nature's greatest gift."

A third violent pain attacked her, and she closed her eyes again, expelling a groan before commencing the measured breathing again. Michael took her hand and held it in his own. She gripped it like a vice and he could see the blood drain from it, as she prevented his circulation process. He felt like groaning, too.

A small sheen of perspiration formed on her forehead and he gently wiped it away with his finger as she continued breathing at a furious rate.

"Hang in, it will pass," he encouraged, but his newfound wisdom came from the experience of witnessing her first bouts of pain.

She said nothing but kept breathing, and then slowly he saw the visible signs of her relaxing slightly and felt her grip on his hand lessen.

"Oh God, that hurt!" she said, opening her eyes.

"I got that impression too." he said, flexing his hand, and they both laughed.

"This differs from the other pains I've had; I reckon the baby wants out now, I'm convinced."

"You can't have it here, we're on a train, in the middle of nowhere," Michael said horrified.

"I don't get to choose when, it doesn't know I'm on a train, does it?"

"It? Don't you know if you're having a boy or a girl, I thought they told you nowadays?"

"They can; my husband and I decided we didn't want to know, we wanted everything to evolve naturally."

"What do you think you're having?"

"I think it's a boy, judging by the way it has kicked me to death for the past couple of months."

"Do you want a boy, or would you prefer a girl?"

"We don't mind, we really don't, as long as it is healthy."

The pain returned. The strength forced her to cry out louder than before. She adopted the same routine, and the circulation recently returned to his hand ceased again.

It took longer for this bout to subside, before she opened her eyes and relaxed her breathing.

"I need the train stopped at the next station and get an ambulance called. Do you think you could arrange that," she asked?

"Anything you need," he promised.

Chapter 35:

"Walk through the carriages, reach the driver, and explain my situation. He'll ensure the train remains there until the ambulance arrives."

Michael stood up, understanding time was crucial, and intending to run through the train. It lurched suddenly, and he lost his balance. Reaching out to grab something; his hand clasped the emergency stop chain. As he fell, the chain followed until the full extent of the slack was exposed. Under his weight, it snapped in two. Immediately, the train braked hard and, the squealing protest of the wheels on the track as they locked, ended any thought of conversation as the train slowed. Michael was thrown forward violently, and without his grip on the chain preventing it, he ended on the floor in a crumpled heap. The train had completely stopped before he stood and checked the woman.

"OOPS," she said and laughed. "I guess we're not waiting for the station. You ok? That was quite a fall?"

"I'm fine, how about you?"

"Ok for the moment," she said.

"Well, I'm afraid we've stopped in the middle of nowhere, not the slightest chance of getting an ambulance here," he told her, staring out the window.

The carriage door opened and a flustered, middle-aged, balding man, bustled through.

"Who pulled the emergency chain?" he asked brusquely.

"I'm afraid I did, but by accident," he looked at Michael angrily.

"I hope you realise, there's a fine for that?" he almost spat out the words.

"Calm down, Harry, stopping the train is the least of our problems. I'm about to have a baby."

"I know, Muriel, that's not the issue, this boy pulled the chain," Harry said, not fully comprehending what she meant.

"Harry, I'm having the baby now, here, on the train, if you don't raise an ambulance."

"Really? Now? Oh!"

"Yes Harry, can you organise an ambulance for me?"

"The next station is about half a mile up the track, I'll get help, you relax, don't move, I'll be back soon. Boy, take care of her, see she gets anything she needs; you hear?"

"Don't worry, I'm not leaving, you can count on me."

"Harry, there's an elderly woman in the first carriage, would you send her to me? And Harry, ask her nicely."

"Leave it to me Muriel, you hang in there."

He uttered his final word as he disappeared through the carriage door.

"Well, you have an advantage over me. You know my name, but I don't know yours," Muriel said, as another spasm of pain gripped her body.

He took her hand, waiting for the pain to subside before telling her his name was Michael. The carriage door opened, and the elderly woman Muriel asked for, entered. She was slightly hunched, moved uneasily, and judging by the number of wrinkles on her face, had to be in her eighties.

"Hello dear," she said, ignoring Michael completely. "I understand you're about to have a baby. I'm Gwen, and I'm looking after you until the ambulance gets here."

"Do you know much about babies?" Michael asked worriedly.

"Had four, so I know enough," she said assuredly. "What's your name, lad?"

"Michael," he told her.

"Michael, can you fetch something for me. A suitcase, two carriages down; fetch it, please. There's clothing in it, we can use to form a makeshift bed on the floor, so she can lie down. I need to prepare her for birth whilst you're gone."

He nodded and ran through the carriages until he found the suitcase and returned with it.

"Open it and spread the clothes on the floor," Gwen commanded, and he responded instantly.

The old lady helped Muriel down, while Michael balled a cardigan, forming a cushion to use as a pillow.

"Her contractions are two minutes apart and decreasing," she told Michael.

"What exactly does that mean?"

"The baby will arrive very soon, hold her hands, give her something to grip when she starts pushing.

" Michael nodded, feeling strangely speechless, and took her hands.

"That job you're going for Michael, perhaps you should reconsider, I'm betting you'll make an excellent midwife."

He laughed, but a realisation dawned in his mind.

"Your last name isn't Stratten, is it?"

"Why yes, how did you know that?"

"The job is on the railways, the person I hoped to meet was M. Stratten. Bert at Ashley station said the M stood for Muriel, oh, and by the way, he sends his best."

"You want to work on the railways? I didn't realise, but the advert has an error, it was supposedly me conducting the interviews, no pun intended, but because the date clashed with my pregnancy due date, it's changed, you should see Douglas Anderson. He works in personnel at Sand Lane Station on the Victoria Line," she ceased talking as the next contraction racked her body.

For half an hour the routine continued, the contractions arriving every two minutes and lasting longer each time. Muriel started to get the urge to push and Gwen told her to resist. Between contractions, Muriel questioned Michael about anything and everything, distracting her mind from the pain and discomfort. He was happy to keep her talking; even though he held her hands, he felt pretty useless and wished he could do more. Speaking of hands, he no longer felt his as they became numb from the tightness of Muriel's grip.

Gwen was amazingly calm. She kept quiet during the conversations between Muriel and Michael, taking charge during the contractions, regulating Muriel's breathing and timing everything. Michael appreciated having her there, thankful he didn't have to care for Muriel alone.

He wondered what was keeping the ambulance men, despite knowing they couldn't get near the train by road. He guessed they were walking trackside from the station. Whatever their reasons it wouldn't make much difference to Muriel, she would have her baby on the train regardless to their imminent arrival, too close to giving birth to be moved now. She had endured so many contractions that Michaels own body clock had become attuned to them. He stiffened himself a few seconds before they arrived. Her grip on his hands during them, tight and painful. Once or twice, he quelled a desire to moan out loud. As the pain increased, so did her moaning and Michael moaned with her.

"What are you doing? Don't tease me, it's not good timing."

"I'm not. When your pain is bad you squeeze my hand harder. You have a stronger grip than Iron Man!"

Muriel laughed despite her pain. "Use this as a lesson, understand the pain a woman endures giving birth."

"Don't worry Muriel I'm a quick learner, so relax your grip whenever."

Muriel laughed again.

"I like you Michael, I could be stuck here with someone a lot less capable. Thanks for your efforts."

"It's a pleasure Muriel, painful, but a pleasure."

The next contraction arrived and Gwen ordered her to push instead of resisting. Michael had never experienced anybody pushing so hard, and the force exerted against him, was so strong he locked his feet against one of the seats to hold her in position. She let out a determined groan of effort each time she pushed, and Gwen announced triumphantly that the baby's head was crowning after the third big effort. She related everything as it happened. Two further huge pushes and the head was completely out.

Gwen explained once the shoulders were through, the rest was easy by comparison. The shoulders emerged, and the remaining followed after two more concerted efforts. A little cry emerged as Gwen lifted the new-born baby and passed her to Muriel.

"Congratulations, my dear. You have a baby daughter and she is positively gorgeous."

Muriel held the baby closely, kissing it on the forehead, while Michael suffered agony from the returning blood supply to his hands.

"Have you chosen a name for her, dear?"

"I hadn't, but I know now. I'm calling her Michaela."

"Thank you, thank you both so much for everything you've done, I couldn't have managed on my own.

"If you want a job as a ticket collector or steward, Michael, I promise I'll make sure you get it. You are the type of person who goes beyond the norm to help others."

The carriage door opened and Harry burst in, followed by two ambulance men.

"Good grief Muriel, couldn't you wait until these guys got here," he said grinning. "Look at the mess that you've made in my carriage."

"Come on Harry, you'll be famous for being the driver of a train with a baby born on it; my guess is you'll be interviewed by the press and appear on the news later."

The ambulance men moved in, unrolling a stretcher and started preliminary checks on Muriel and her baby.

"We had a lengthy walk getting here, which means we have quite a walk to reach our ambulance. It might be a little uncomfortable. The trolley is no use on the tracks, so we're doing this the old-style. The good news is that you've saved us a fair amount of work already. Now, if you guys will leave us, I'd like to examine both of my patients properly before moving them."

Gwen and Michael waited further down the carriage for them to finish and one told them they were about to leave. Michael walked alongside them to the station, and then to the ambulance before mother and baby were loaded on board. Muriel called him before they left, asking him to bend down so they could talk discretely. He did as she requested, and she kissed him on the cheek.

"I don't really have anything to say except thank you, but I know you teenagers don't like receiving affection from olds, it's not cool, is it?"

They said their goodbyes quickly, and he walked back onto the station to complete his journey although now the destination had changed. He needed Sand Lane Station on the Victoria Line to get the job offer Muriel promised was his.

Chapter 36:

Michael sat, waiting for Harry's train to arrive, it had remained stationary for some time and he needed to return to it, to reach London. Reviewing the events of the past couple of hours, he realised he experienced a privileged preview of what most fathers would be involved with at the birth of their child. He felt honoured and special; she named the baby girl after him. He considered her promise of a job, hoping Douglas Anderson would view him as positive a candidate for employment as she had.

Wow! Today had certainly been a little different and special he thought; with only one exception, the job hunting had become positive, he had met decent people and couldn't wait to tell his mother and Mary when returning.

A humming on the track, broke through his thoughts and he glanced up to see the train arriving. He glimpsed Harry's face through the window, and he raised his hand as he passed by, bringing the train to a halt. Michael noticed the grin on his face, understanding he had enjoyed contributing.

Michael boarded a different carriage and sat down, noticing he was completely alone again on the carriage. As soon as the train left the station, he wondered what else could happen. Everything was so out of the ordinary, quite bizarre.

Surprisingly, rest of the journey was uneventful, but mercifully peaceful, and he relaxed, enjoying the swaying motion of the train, until finally stopping at Derrybrook station. He sought information regarding the location of the underground.

Unlike Ashley, this station buzzed with people, bees around a nest, and he waited in line to show his ticket and leave. He asked a railway employee for directions to the underground and he suggested taking the number six bus from outside the station. He moved quickly, free from the queue, but with no chance of catching the bus, he had no money.

The typical red of the London busses was easy to recognise, and as the number six approached, he noted the names of its main stops and started walking. Surely, there would be underground stations everywhere. He only had to ask someone. Every Londoner would know where the tube stations were. Michael walked for fifteen minutes before seeing the underground sign up ahead. He increased his pace, despite being in no hurry.

The town heaved with people. The station might be smaller than the more renown destinations, but the town was larger than Bert had suggested. It was worse than Ashley on market day. It reminded him of his vision and the masses in the tunnel, though not quite as bad. Covering the few steps needed to reach the overhead sign stating the Victoria Line, he noticed a flight of steps below. Whatever he expected, it wasn't a staircase leading below the pavement, despite making perfect sense for an underground train station.

He paused, knowing he had time. It had been ages since his last drink, and the café across the road looked inviting. He checked the change in his pocket and hoped a tea wouldn't cost more in London than Ashley.

Crossing the road seemed a lottery fraught with danger. People were crossing everywhere, stopping mid-road after negotiating the first lane of traffic, before taking on the opposite stream. The vehicles didn't slow for them. Michael took his chance, adopting the same strategy for crossing as the locals and miraculously achieving it without injury. He paused at the café, checking the price list on the door before entering.

He sat at a table, ordering a tea when the waitress came across. There was no conversation, just a perfunctory service. Michael watched life happening through the window. The pace frenetic, everyone on a mission to get somewhere fast. He wasn't comfortable with it. They were so busy they were existing rather than living. He was breathless watching it. His tea arrived, and apart from his thanks, no other word was spoken. He believed Londoners were supposedly friendly, no evidence of that present. He drank his tea and continued to watch outside.

Five minutes later, Michael risked crossing the road again and walked the few paces to the tube station entrance.

Descending rapidly, he was aware the steps were wide, each holding several people simultaneously. He couldn't remember steps like these anywhere in Ashley. At the bottom, slightly to the left, a ticket office, already with a queue of a dozen people waiting, and he took position at the rear. *Sand Lane Station,* he reminded himself of his destination. When his turn arrived, he ordered his ticket after explaining he was attending an interview. He was instructed to seek platform five. *How big was this place,* he wondered, searching for a sign pointing to the Victoria Line?

He was in luck, spotting one immediately, and walked confidently towards it, following the wide walking space, reminding him of the subway in Ashley under the main road. He was awed at the mass of humanity here. It seemed peculiar, they all head in the same direction, before reasoning there was a different route for those leaving the station. Further ahead, a sign showing platforms one to four with an arrow pointing right, and an arrow pointing left for platforms five and six. He went left and immediately descended to a lower level.

The steps led into a tunnel with dirty white tiles on the walls. People crammed in, grains of sugar in a two-kilo bag, and after walking the few steps towards them, the pace of his movement slowed dramatically. Pressure from behind, and restricted space in front, controlled his speed. People jostled and pushed, trying to force their way ahead of those in front, but space to move into was non-existent, and they remained in position, moving the same pace as everybody else. A rush of air whistled down the tunnel lifting the fringe from his forehead, it wasn't fresh, heavily laden with the stench of soot. The overweight man in front walked with a swagger, swinging one leg forward followed by the other. At that instant of recognition, he realised he'd been here before, seen this before, experienced this before.

Chapter 37:

A moment of panic. Michael sought to turn, push through the crowd of people, up the stairs and the fresh air above. He could walk to Sand Lane Station, better than this! As he turned his head to check his escape route, the mass of people behind suggested his idea was impossible. No choice, he was forced to proceed with everybody else.

He relived his visions for the next few minutes, following the familiar route, reaching the bottom of the stairs, and coming to a halt after a few more steps. The sound and rush of wind whooshed over him, and those in front moved forward. Everything from his visions were clear now. It seemed obvious, the sound of the underground train, and the wind, the air that it pushed along the track in front.

Michael stood in a large area between two platforms, one on each side of him. He asked a man behind which was platform five, and he pointed to his left rather than shouting an answer. Michael turned slightly, facing it, even though it remained unseen through the bodies ahead.

Minutes of waiting passed, and a rush of wind announced the arrival of another train. It arrived and those in front edged forward. With the sudden thinning out of the crowd in front, Michael stared in horror at a train, so full of people they could not move, invading one another's personal space. *Sardines in a tin! How could anybody travel like this, it's inhuman he thought?* The doors closed without an inch of wasted space and the train sped off. In front of the masses now, his turn boarding the next train was imminent.

A woman carrying a small infant stood next to him looking flustered and unhappy. She put the infant down and shook her arms to gain feeling back into them. She grabbed the child's hand, keeping him close to her. She needn't have worried; the child was terrified, and Michael empathised with his feelings. He clung to his mother's leg with his free hand, wrapping his arm almost completely around it. The child needed a buggy, but using a buggy in this crowd was impossible.

He peered at the faces of the people, waiting impatiently, they were many nationalities here, more than he'd witnessed in one place and he discerned a range of unknown languages being spoken. The volume of conversation was huge, seeming to blend into a type of white noise, used to torture prisoners in a film he'd watched at the cinema. The noise turned on when the prisoners tried to sleep.

The smell of soot was powerful, an assault on the nose, inviting you want to pinch it to prevent it penetrating into the throat. He couldn't wait to leave here. Suddenly, a surge from behind propelled him forward with irresistible force; he almost fell over the edge of the platform, onto the track below. Others at the front almost followed the same fate. The woman with the child screamed; the most awful, desperate scream imaginable.

She shouted. "My baby, my baby!"

Michael glanced down, where the child had stood, His tiny space now empty. The mother pointed downward, hands over her mouth, eyes wild with fright and desperation. Michael peered over the edge of the platform and saw the child laying prone in the gap between the nearest rail and the side wall. He didn't consider his next actions. He just acted. Launching himself off the platform, he landed squarely on his feet between the rails.

"Don't touch the rails," somebody shouted.

Michael was already aware of the consequences of that. He moved closer to the child before stepping over the rail separating them. He hadn't moved and Michael guessed he had landed hard, possibly unconscious; He hoped it was nothing worse than that. He lifted him gently and raised him up. Several pairs of hands lowered, taking the child; a whoosh of wind struck his face, the instant the weight of the child passed to those above. Michael noticed a small toy at his feet. Believing it belonged to the child, he stooped to gather it. He failed to hear the cries of get out after spotting two stickers on the toy. The letters G and E distracting his attention. He lifted his head in time to see a train bearing down. No time to react, no time to experience fear. He closed his eyes.

Waiting to feel the inevitable impact, nothing happened. He had spotted the train a microsecond distant, instantly knowing the time for escape was impossible. Even with his eyes closed, he braced for the impact not daring to open them; still it didn't come. The voices, shouting for him to get out, had ceased; he couldn't discern a single sound. Strange! Not what he expected.

Forcing himself to open his eyes, he discovered everything was blurred, he had screwed them shut so tightly, it blurred his vision and his eyes were awash with additional fluid. Waiting for them to clear seemed like an eternity, but as he rubbed them gently, his vision started to return.

He noticed he no longer stood, but sat on a bench in the High Street in Ashley. *That's different,* he thought. The busker was playing something modern for a change. Michael recognised it as an Ed Shearon number. The man nodded towards him and Michael returned it, before checking his watch and noticing it was nine o'clock. *Really, again?* He asked an elderly woman who happened to be passing by. She looked familiar.

"Sorry love, but what day of the week is it, I seem to have got my days muddled?" Michael asked.

"Don't worry love, I do that all the time, but today is Tuesday, and it's Tuesday all day."

"Thanks."

"Merry Christmas."

"Same to you."

Michael pulled the card from his shirt pocket and opened it out. The card was completed. The letters G and E already stuck in, this time he had no recollection of how. Closing it, he placed it back in his pocket and tried to reason again what everything meant. His brain wouldn't work, and no thoughts emerged from it.

The nauseas feeling, experienced before, returned, and he shut his eyes, taking deep breaths. It was stronger, and he was convinced he would vomit. He became aware the busker had ceased singing, and then a hand rested on his shoulder.

"You all right lad?" The busker asked.

"I think so, nauseous."

"Take a few deep breaths lad, it always helps."

Michael followed the advice, and felt the queasiness subside. He concentrated on the breathing and nothing else.

Chapter 38:

The sickness passed shortly, and Michael focused on what he saw in his vision. Except, he was no longer sure it was a vision. It was, and it wasn't. What was real, some of it? Any of it, all of it? Was it simply a dream, because here he sat, in Ashley, listening to his favourite busker? He had lost time, again, why? And, why always returning to the same time, and day? So weird.

Another thought became apparent. Was this all a premonition? Was he seeing the future? It made sense in some ways. Why more events were revealed each vision was odd. Surely, if a premonition, the entire events would be exposed in one, not like a tv series. If it was the future being revealed, why experience it frequently and then return home.

Michael was getting increasingly confused, frustrated because the answers weren't obvious. *Time to see Mary,* he thought. He could only share this with her; she wouldn't laugh at him, and trusted him enough to believe him. He wondered how he would have coped without her these past weeks; she was a tower of strength, despite crediting him for saving her. He was fortunate to have her.

Had he really known her for weeks? It seemed like it, but because he kept returning to Tuesday the reality suggested it was less than a week. Unless, of course, he returned to different Tuesdays, but that was improbable, it was still the Christmas period every time. What a mess!

Walking down the Lower High Street, he realised although only a few days before Christmas, the lack of a festive feeling still existed. Despite his recent experiences, he wasn't concerned about himself, he had questions that he desperately wanted answering, but at least these visions no longer panicked him. He wanted to accept it as a dream, but it was too simple an explanation, the events were too complicated to dismiss as a dream.

Entering the Wimpy, he picked her out of a sea of waitresses easily. Clearly, the short staffing period had finished. It was Tuesday, the reason so many members of staff were on duty, was unclear. Perhaps staff training, or maybe an event in town, was attracting additional people. If so, they would expect to be busy. He called her name, and she turned. Instantly, her warm, welcoming smile transformed her face. He had become used to seeing it and experiencing its calming effect.

"Morning, Michael, I wondered if you would visit today. I hoped so, but thought it would be in later in the day. It's a lovely surprise to see you this early."

"I need to discuss everything that's happened since I saw you last. You won't believe what happened."

"That sounds exciting, but I don't have a break for ages."

"Eleven o'clock?"

"Yes."

"Oh well, I'll sit here drinking tea and pass the time until your break."

"Wow, I'll accept it as a compliment, you being prepared to wait for me that long."

"Well, you're my best friend."

"I like that, you're mine too."

"As much as I enjoy seeing you smile Mary, you just going to stand there, or make me a tea?"

Mary blushed! "Cheeky!" She disappeared and returned shortly, with a tea and another smile. Michael couldn't help but reciprocate, her smiles always invoked a similar response.

"Why so many staff today, Mary?"

"Staff training, the recent period of short staffing, due to sickness, inspired the boss to employ more."

"Sensible."

She went back to the kitchen, leaving him with his thoughts.

One and a half hours to wait, a long time, but Michael wanted to explore his recent events to ensure he hadn't missed or forgotten anything. Despite being a repetitive dream or a series of visions, it felt real. Possibly, he might answer one of his questions after thinking harder about it. It was not his imagination, but every time he woke from a vision, he was close to the employment office. The same woman revealed the day, every time he posed the question? Following that, he walked into the High Street and encountered the busker.

He smiled ruefully; this was supposed to connect pieces of the jigsaw, but raised more questions.

The hour and a half passed quicker than he expected, and Mary slid into the seat opposite.

"Are you still coming to dinner on Sunday?"

"Of course."

"Good, my Gran wants to thank you again for Charlie."

"Appreciated, but not required."

"So, spill the beans, what's happened?"

Michael relayed everything he could remember, every single detail of the train journey and helping Muriel with the birth.

"Wow! Michael, I'm so jealous, things happen around you. What an amazing experience. You witnessed and helped at a birth, and the child was named after you. That's so cool."

"You think that was cool, wait until you hear what happened next. I had another vision, and it took me further than before; I think it's the ending."

The next part of his story took longer than Mary had left of her break. Her boss sought her out.

"Mary, break's over, you're needed in the kitchen," he said coldly.

"I'm afraid I'm not on my break, this young man is unwell, he needs help. He needs home, or the doctors. He's already passed out once, I should help him home."

"Mary, we can't afford you having time off now."

"Perhaps you could pay for a taxi to get him home?"

"Mmm, can you take him home and return in half an hour?"

"I reckon so. Where do you live, Michael?"

Michael played along with the ruse. "It's the other side of town, twenty minutes' walk each way. Urgh! I think I'm going to vomit."

"Get him outside quickly, Mary, before he's sick in here."

Mary made a show of helping Michael outside, moving away down the street before bursting out laughing.

"You're so bad, Mary, that was brilliant acting."

"I want to hear the rest of your story now! I can't wait another two and a half hours."

Michael led her to a bench and, once seated, he completed the story.

"Oh! Goodness Michael, it's horrible. I was unsure what to expect; it wasn't that."

"The question is, what now? If it's the end what was the purpose? This will plague me for ages without answers."

"I've no suggestions yet, but I reckon doing something will distract your mind from everything."

"What should I do? It's Tuesday, again, and you're working, I've no money for anything else."

"The office, where you met Brian, is open; you could visit him. You've filled the card in."

"It's an idea, but I'm not sure of his working hours, or if I can see him without an appointment."

"I remember you telling me, he was an independent, he'll need to work if he's self-employed."

"Yes, he is. You're right. He might see me."

"If you're going to visit him now, take a detour past the Wimpy, I don't want that skinflint boss of mine seeing you."

Michael grinned. "Right, I'll do that and I'll see you later, after your shift, and walk you home."

"I'd enjoy that, but if not, I'll see you tomorrow."

Mary hugged him before she left. He was becoming accustomed to her affectionate ways, deciding he enjoyed their closeness.

Chapter 39:

Michael took an alley to avoid the Wimpy and head towards the offices. He passed the busker in the Upper High Street and exchanged customary nods. A short walk from there to the employment office followed. It remained ugly when he arrived, not that he expected any change. As he entered the building into the foyer, his head started pounding. He looked for a sign signifying washroom and spotting it,, followed the guiding arrow.

Entering, Michael went straight to the sink and ran the cold water. Splashing some on his face, he felt the coldness invigorate him a little. He sipped some, but it tasted disgusting, his mother advised drinking plenty of water with a headache in case of dehydration. Michael never argued with advice from her, it was always good.

Outside the waiting area there was a water dispenser near the entrance door and after towelling off Michael walked to it. He placed a plastic cup under, pulled the small lever forward, and watched the water fill it. He gulped it down even though freezing cold. Immediately, he felt the pounding ease, and poured a second cup to take with him.

Returning to the receptionist, he asked to see Brian Maxwell.

"Do you have an appointment?"

"No, he suggested he was always available."

She picked up the telephone, pressed a button and waited for him to reply.

"Mr Maxwell, I've a young man who wants to see you, regarding tasks you set him.

"What's your name?" she asked, placing her hand over the mouth piece, so she wasn't overheard.

"Michael Ferguson," he told her, and she relayed his name to Brian before replacing the phone on its holder.

"Mr Maxwell will see you, but has a fairly full list of appointments. It might be a while before he fits you in. If you wait on the fifth floor, he'll call you as soon as possible."

Michael thanked her and climbed the five flights of stairs leading to the waiting room. Entering, he sat in the same seat he had occupied during his last visit. The digital clock clicked away and the rotating digits turned one at a time. 8:58, 8:59, 9:00... That's weird, it was 9:00 when he checked his watch on bench before visiting Mary, and that was hours ago. Time had vanished from his memory again, and this he had no recollection of anything happening, except... except the headache, did that trigger time loss? Surely not.

Everything appeared as before, a procession of people entering all the doors except six, the one he expected to use. The people looked similar, or was it just déjà vu? He'd experienced that frequently of late. Finally, and without having glued his attention to the digits on the clock, door six opened. He checked the time, wanting to know how long he had waited, not that it really mattered. 9:00! Strange! Time stood still. Brian appeared, dressed and moving in the same meticulous manner he had before.

"I wasn't expecting you so soon Michael, come through and take a seat."

Michael followed him into his office and sat on the same hard plastic chair. He was feeling uneasy with all this 'same' business.

"I've been hearing good things about you, young man, you've been making good impressions on everybody you've met recently."

"How do you know that?" Michael asked.

"The coded letters you've been collecting recently, every time one is given, part of the agreement with prospective employers, is for them to give me feedback on your interviews. It allows me to track your efforts and progress in finding work. You are very proactive, young man, and your success rate, extremely high. For every job you applied for, with one exception, you were given two letters. That's rare, extremely rare. Normally a candidate gets one per job, occasionally two, if they make a real impact, but two in each case, well it's special, very special. So, tell me about each vacancy you applied for and I'll share the feedback I received in each case."

Michael wasn't expecting that. A system for Brian to receive feedback was sensible, but he held doubts about the system until now. Seemed it was more effective than he suspected. But for him to share the feedback was a bonus. He could learn from this.

He explained events leading to the demise of the newspaper Brian gave to him, stating most of the adverts were totally unreadable. Brian empathised, suggesting it did not matter since there were sufficient left to attend interviews and gain the stickers he required. Explaining Mary's way of gaining employment, through offering free trials, Brian seemed impressed, especially after Michael tried it with success at the RSPCA office. Sharing the story about the injured dog, and how the vet helped it, Michael explained its injury was mild concussion. The idea to place it with Mary and her lonely Gran came during his shift there. Michael's enthusiasm, while sharing the story, increased during it. It was a job he could excel at. Worthwhile, and it helped creatures and people alike.

"I spoke to the vet earlier, you really impressed him, and at this moment, you're the clear favourite for a permanent job."

"That's pleasing to hear, I enjoyed working there. Bruce said the job was mine after the first shift." he said, pleased with the report Brian had given him. "I never managed a second shift there. Something kept happening that I'll explain later."

Michael told him about Mr Jollie at the Tuck Shop next. He kept the report short, stating he was interested in the job and thought shifts there might fill the hours not utilised at the RSPCA job. Combined, the two jobs would have enough hours to make the working week full.

"More happened there, didn't it? I have spoken to Mr Jollie, and he told me you played an instrumental part in breaking up a shop lifting racket. Apparently, older boys were forcing younger children to steal for them so that they could sell the goods to make money. You helped a young lad called Tom admit what he was being forced to do and then catch the true thieves. You helped the other boys too, despite not having any real involvement with them directly. Mr Jollie was so grateful for your efforts, and the way you conducted yourself; you're a clear favourite for this job too."

"It was decent of him to give such good feedback; I really appreciate it. Michael responded.

"You were injured after; took a beating from friends of the arrested youths?"

Michael didn't answer, only Mary knew that. The man who helped him? They hadn't exchanged details. He fell silent confused and a little concerned.

Brian noticed his discomfort and reverted to something more positive.

"What job did you go for next?" Brian asked.

"The next job was interesting and unexpected. Once there, I discovered the position was for a Fosser. I had no idea what a Fosser was. I expected the job to be landscaping. Once I learnt the details about , it interested me the most. I like the idea of working outside in a beautiful and peaceful location. Perhaps no opportunity for a career advancement, but the satisfaction of caring for the cemetery would be huge. Talking to and comforting grieving relatives has to be worthwhile, and David suggested he'd made countless friends there. I really liked him, one of the most caring, decent people I've ever met; working with him would be cool."

"How do you feel about digging graves for people who have died?"

"It doesn't worry me; we all end up six feet under eventually, so to speak. I'd ensure the graves I dig would be as perfect as possible. Everybody deserves the best after living their lives in a challenging world. The prospect of working the grounds is amazing, the workload is heavy to keep it as lovely as possible, and David's pride in that was clear to see."

"His pride is always evident; well, it's probably of no surprise to you I've spoken to him already. Once again, you had a positive impact. He liked your attitude, especially your patience and care, towards one of the grievers at the cemetery. I believe Jennifer was her name.

He considers you the perfect candidate for the job and asked me to withdraw the advert from circulation. The job is yours as far as he's concerned."

Michael beamed with pleasure, pleased with the report that David had given. He moved on to the next of his applications.

"The next place I visited was the sports centre for a coaching position. It was the most unusual interview I had. I had to play badminton with Terry, the senior sports coach, and then table tennis, so he understood the level I played at. He had a training commitment with somebody my age called Lee, and I helped him warm-up and was invited to coach both through their match. My efforts and advice pleased him; he said I could consider myself interviewed and didn't have to attend a formal one except for the paperwork. I thought the opportunities for a career in coaching seemed promising and although I was personally satisfied with everything, it didn't quite match the level I achieved at the cemetery.

"You did please him, Michael. I spoke to him earlier and again you job is yours for the taking. He was particularly pleased with how you helped Lee. The lad apparently had issues to resolve, beyond the remit of a coach. The advice you gave Lee helped him make some major decisions and is changing his life. Well done, Michael. When I met you, the first time, you stated you weren't making impact at interviews and was never offered employment. What changed, what attributed to all this sudden success?

"I wondered that myself. Meeting my new friend, Mary, was such a positive event. I had no friends left before her. The success at the RSPCA gave me confidence, but mostly, meeting a succession of cool and decent people at the interviews was great. They all cared, showed interest, and were positive. I guess that positivity rubbed off."

Where did you go next?"

"I went to arrange an interview at the Post Office next, but unfortunately never achieved it. I filled in application forms and left them, but the person in charge of viewing applicants was absent sick. This was my least successful attempt. Impressing somebody and making myself known there, I failed."

"Well, you actually impressed others unconnected to Royal Mail, Michael. I received a phone call from a friend, Reverend Green, from St Mary's Parish Church in town. He explained the help you gave an elderly parishioner called Lucy. You carried a parcel from the sorting office for her, and helped her become positive about moving home. The Reverend is friendly with the recruitment officer at the sorting office, he is recommending you, as a thank you.

"That's decent of him. If I see him, I'll thank him."

"And now your last interview."

"Something weird happened, and I never quite finished the process.

"What do you mean?"

"Well, it started well. I met Muriel, the woman the advert suggested speaking to, but things happened. The job was about becoming a steward or ticket collector on the railways; I actually met Muriel on the train to London. She told me of a mistake in the advert. She was relieved from the task because she was pregnant and the date of the interviews clashed with her having a baby. To shorten the story, I needed to cross London and meet a man called Douglas Anderson. I never finished the trip. An incident on the underground prevented the rest of my journey, and suddenly I was back in Ashley. I don't understand what happened. It's as if I lost my memory. The stickers suggest I attended the interview. To be honest, I feel like a fraud."

"Don't concern yourself with that, Michael, because you deserve more than stickers for your efforts. I believe I am correct in suggesting strange events happened to you, since engaging with my special vacancies, and you've experienced difficulties understanding them."

Michael was stunned into silence; how could Brian know anything about that?

Chapter 40:

"How can you know?" Michael asked, amazed at his apparent knowledge of what had happened.

"Oh, there's a reason behind everything that happens, but you realise that already, don't you?"

"Well, that's what I've always believed; it's what my mother taught me."

"Your mother is a fine woman, very astute."

"You know my mother?" Michael asked incredulously.

"Not personally, but I have knowledge of her and other members of your family. The explanation will become clear later, may be unnecessary after you fully comprehend what happened."

"What happened, what am I missing?" Michael asked worriedly.

"The reason you've received those images was deliberate. Hopefully to lessen the shock of reality when full understanding occurs. It's traumatic for many to accept reality, and visions can help, especially when the revelations are unpleasant. Sit back and close your eyes, Michael. Allow the truth to be revealed."

Was it an instruction or a request? Michael wasn't sure, and it didn't really matter. He couldn't remember the last time he went to bed. Bed had been missing for a week.

Closing his eyes, he found himself back in the tube station waiting for the train to Sand Lane Station. As before, woman and child stood next to him. The child had one hand firmly gripped in his mother's and the other arm wrapped around her leg. The underground was an absolutely frightening place for a child that age.

He felt the surge of pressure behind and struggled to prevent himself falling on the tracks. The woman next to him screamed. He looked down, seeing the child had disappeared, but knowing where he was. Jumping down between the tracks, he made his way towards him, being careful not to touch the live rail. Gently, he raised him to the outstretched hands, and felt the relief of his weight disappear as he was clutched from above.

A rush of wind roared past, but he ignored it as he bent to pick up the child's toy, noticing the two stickers on it. The G and the E almost glowed as he spotted them, distracting him from reality. He realised he had a full set for his card.

Smiling, he glanced up, and saw the train bearing down. He knew what it meant, understood what was about to happen. There was nothing to prevent the inevitable. Time froze momentarily. He hadn't shared his successes from the past few days with his family, hadn't shared about the people he had met. About to die, and they would never realise his success. He closed his eyes again and for the tiniest fraction of a second, he felt the trains touch, not the impact he expected, just a gentle caress. Experiencing the sensation of flying, the images darkened, and he opened his eyes.

Still sitting in the office, he hadn't moved. Brian had not moved either, staring at him with compassion adorning his face. Instantly alert and focussed, he knew beyond doubt what had happened to him, but if true, where was he now?

"Do you understand Michael... understand why you couldn't remember gaining the last two letters."

"I couldn't remember the last interview, it never happened, I never reached there. I died, didn't I? I mean I am dead now, aren't I?"

He looked at Brian's face for confirmation. It wasn't there at first. Then a single tear rolled gently down Brian's cheek.

"Forgive me," he said. "I have never mastered the control of my emotions when somebody receives the light of awareness." He nodded an affirmation; he was right and was dead in the physical sense.

"I'll never see my mother or my family again, will I?" he asked, feeling the first tug of emotion, a powerful sadness swarming through him.

"Oh yes, Michael, yes you will, frequently and whenever you want, but you can't communicate as in the physical world."

Michael refrained from talking, allowing the revelation he was dead, and the realisation he no longer belonged in the physical world, sink in.

"So, who or what are you, Brian? an angel or something similar?" Michael asked.

"No, I'm not an angel; that right belongs to a select few. No, I'm known as a seeker. It's a couple of steps down from an angel. My role is to vet candidates passing to the afterlife. Discovering where they would be best employed in heaven."

Employed? You work in heaven?"

"Of course, everybody has a role of some sort; everybody contributes to the common cause, so to speak. We don't get paid, unlike the physical world, but there are benefits far beyond, and you'll soon start learning about them when you finally leave this office."

"So, you're telling me, everything I've experienced was fabricated, so you can select the role I'm best suited for. All the amazing people I've met weren't real, or at best, were dead, and everything recently didn't happen."

"No, not at all, everything you've done, since meeting me, and most of the people you've talked to, seen and helped, live in the physical world, their problems were real and your help changed their lives."

Michael was struggling to accept Brian's revelations, regarding who was alive and who was dead. He couldn't work it out, experiencing the same confusion he had with the visions.

"How could anything I did change their lives? If I was dead, how could they see and talk to me?"

"Let's start with now Michael. At this point, you're dead, but your spirit remains in limbo before journeying to heaven. That's because your vocation isn't decided. It's my role to help you with that, everyone must have a role suiting their best potential, and something that satisfies. As you've not crossed, I, as the seeker, have powers to return you to the physical world to complete tasks revealing your true potential. Do you understand, so far?"

"I think so," he answered.

"Your life in the physical world centred round finding work for twelve months, so that's the area I selected for you to continue with. Every person who visits me, the situation I place them in is different, based solely on their most recent experiences. This is the first time I've evaluated anyone at a job centre.

It all sounded surreal. If he understood this correctly, he was apparently being interviewed for a position in his spiritual existence, simultaneously to being interviewed for positions in his physical existence. Bizarre and sort of cool, too.

Chapter 41:

"Now let's discuss the changes you've made to other's lives. Every event or spoken word impacts somebody, but in our physical life we rarely consider that. Honestly, it's far easier to observe this in our spirit state. Your kindness towards Mary is not surprising when you learn who she is, or rather who she was. Mary died at birth nineteen years ago, the same day as you were born. You had a natural affinity with her, comfortable close from the beginning.

Perhaps what I reveal next is the second most difficult reality you have to accept, Michael. Mary is an accurate representation of your twin sister who was stillborn. You had no knowledge of having a twin, your brother and sister also had no knowledge. Your parents took her loss hard and decided not to share their loss with the three of you."

Brian paused, allowing him to absorb the information.

"You say she's an accurate representation?"

"Yes."

"It answers many confusing questions I had about her. I liked her, a lot, but not as a potential girlfriend. I wondered why, she looks good and has a lovely personality, but I told myself my focus was all about finding work. I never seemed to have enough time with her. My poor parents.

"You'll have plenty of time in the future Michael, she waits for you as we speak."

"And her grandmother?"

"A part played by another from upstairs."

Michael nodded, accepting what Brian told him was becoming easier.

"The dog you helped, Charlie, was real. He went to a decent owner who loved to dance. The dog learned to dance too and they perform in public. Together they become so adept, they earn a living from it."

"All the jobs you sought were fabricated to allow you opportunity to help others, to alter their lives for the better. Of course, despite presenting the opportunities I had no idea how many of them you would implement.

"With Mr Jollie and Tom, the focus was Tom. Mr Jollie already has everything from life he wanted, and was content, but Tom had real problems. Once the bullies were removed, he changes completely, becomes confident and hard-working, he will achieve great things. He, and his sister form a business in their teens and make a fortune by their late twenties. Using their vast wealth, they instigate a children's charity specialising in helping the young, suffering from bullying. They operate similar to Childline and work at this until they retire."

"I didn't realise the power of influence individuals have, or how easy it is to alter someone's direction, good or bad," Michael said, surprised at the impact he had made.

"How could you, none of this has happened yet? In the spiritual world, what happens on Earth, has happened, is happening, or will happen, we choose what to witness. To truly assess a person's potential, we learn how to influence others; manipulating time is an essential part of what I do."

"I understand, I think!"

"Oh, the best is yet to come. Jennifer, what a difference belief in somebody makes, Michael; that's the gift you gave her. In all your conversations, you encouraged her follow her dreams, do what she excelled and loved doing, although her family were against her. The idea of a studio you orchestrated, turned out so successful, she not only paints but writes there too. In time, she writes a couple of dozen best sellers. She and David fall in love and marry in ten years' time, after his first wife suffers and dies from cancer.

"Wow!"

"Now, Lee the table tennis player who because of his talent was forced to play the sport beyond his liking. He takes your advice and pursues a teaching career and specialises in children with behavioural difficulties. Has a positive effect on many. He goes beyond the norm, just like the teacher who influenced him. To achieve this, he coaches table tennis players at a very high level, bringing top athletes into his school to meet and encourage the children. I told you it gets better."

Michael was pleased he had helped people to a degree beyond what he had originally considered. He liked how it made him feel, how it softened the realisation of being dead. But one question he waited to ask, had no resemblance to what Brian revealed.

"This is better than adjusting to being dead.

"Don't worry about being dead Michael, once you've seen upstairs, the effect is astonishing, coming to terms with it is almost immediate, especially when you learn what waits for you."

It sounded intriguing, and he wanted to learn more immediately, what was his role in heaven? but he wanted to learn more about others he had met recently. And then, that question he wanted answering.

"Tell me about Muriel and baby Michaela," he asked him, wanting to learn their future.

"Hang on, there's somebody else whose life you touched, before coming to Muriel. You said you were unsuccessful with the postman position. In terms of the job, you were correct, but your effect on Lucy was successful. The underlying task was to find her contentment and happiness; You helped with her independence. Deciding to move into a home, of her own volition, was all she needed. In the care home you visited with her, she finds herself valued and respected.

She lives to an incredible one-hundred and seven years old and gets her telegram from the queen. She remains there for her life's duration and befriends the woman in charge. Together they make changes to how the elderly are cared for. This benefits not only those living there, but also influences similar changes in other care homes. They will write a successful book on how to care and respect the elderly, Jennifer at the cemetery helps them. It becomes a best seller in its field and helps their work reach a wider audience.

"That's pretty cool too, I wasn't expecting that."

"Now Muriel, and baby Michaela. Muriel is another fortunate person, happy as she is; her husband also. They remain working for the railway for all their working life and have four children on route, ha, no pun intended. Their first, Michaela, will become an international singing star. From a young age, she shows a rare ability to play any instrument, has a voice that people to listen to, and words reaching them at deeper levels. Despite her fame and fortune, she remains the same gentle person her mother is, happy and content, and able to find peace away from the media circus generally following such stars. Without your involvement at her birth Muriel, would have collapsed on the train, and the baby stillborn."

That revelation stunned Michael especially after learning about his twin who suffered that fate. He reminded Brian that Gwen was present too and was more instrumental during the birthing process than he, so even in his absence Gwen would have been present.

"Gwen wasn't... Well, explaining about Gwen easily, requires understanding that Gwen wasn't who she appeared to be. She was sent by us to help you with the birth, it was unfair and unrealistic of us to expect a nineteen-year-old boy to have enough experience of child birth to cope alone in that situation."

"So, Gwen wasn't Gwen at all?"

"Oh, she was Gwen, but her role in life, or should I say the afterlife, differs from the impression she might have given, but I'll explain more later.

"Now, the last person you helped was the mother and baby, ultimately leading to your death. The woman is a devout Christian who spends her entire life abroad working as a missionary. Her child, her only, grows up and becomes a dedicated preacher who ministers in the public eye. He raises extortionate amounts of money throughout his life and spends it all on worthwhile causes around the world, keeping only the bare minimum to scratch out a humble living. He influences thousands of people worldwide to take up Christianity and acts as an ambassador in several important peace talks designed at ending conflict between warring factions. Saving his life, Michael leads to thousands of others being saved during the next sixty years of his life."

Michael held up his hand to stop Brian continuing. The question on his mind now dominating his thoughts.

"I need to know, Brian, why I'm not feeling emotional about leaving my family and friends behind. I mean I love them all. Why don't I feel upset losing them?"

"You're not losing them Michael, passing to heaven allows all to take their family members essences with them. The memories are complete in your spiritual mind; you see them as clearly as in the physical world.

"Those dying momentarily, and then returning, claim their life flashes through their mind, they see their families and moments from their physical lives. It's true. The time between dying and ascending to heaven is unlimited. You're experiencing that now and have been for a while.

Throughout this process, you had memories of your past with each significant family member. It shows they never fade away; you never forget. It prevents you from enduring the grief they suffer after you died. You must cope with moving forward and assuming a position of importance."

"I wish they didn't have to suffer."

"It's a process all experience in the physical world, feelings define who you are, who they are, don't wish to deprive them, it strengthens them, makes them grow."

"I want to know why I suffered so much misery at the start? I was experiencing it when you interviewed me. You could have prevented that."

"Michael, you must experience the bad to recognise the good. Consider how much you've grown. Out of the ashes… a rebirth, so to speak. Despite feeling so desperate, you gained strength, and self-worth from helping others.

Chapter 42:

Brian paused with his explanations to allow Michael an opportunity to ask any further questions. Michael stared at him. The man was experiencing emotion; a satisfaction, perhaps an excitement. The reason eluded him, but the smile suggested something. Michael sat back in his chair, welcoming the break in the onslaught of revelations, and considering the purpose behind them.

"So, all those jobs were real, yes?" he broke the temporary silence, to seek further confirmation.

"They were real, you would have achieved offers of employment from all, had you lived."

"They seem unrelated, how do they connect to give you the information about my employment in heaven?"

"The jobs are unrelated. The hidden tasks within each, provided the key information about what you're suited for."

"You mean the helping people bit."

"Exactly! Are you aware, during the time you pursued job, and helped others, all you requested for yourself, was a cup of tea? You helped everyone, asking for nothing in return.

"So, what's my destiny then."

"I'm waiting for confirmation from upstairs for the recommendation I've made, it shouldn't take long but you can't leave before it comes."

Michael nodded. "Sounds as if the job I'll have is important and I appreciate that, I'd hate something boring."

"Oh, it certainly won't be boring, Michael, and I'm know it involves helping people."

"That's cool, a job with a feel-good factor."

Michael's demeanour had changed. He was unaware. He now accepted everything Brian revealed, and now all he was concerned about was his new job. He felt no pride for his achievements, helping others is what he did, like the majority of his family. Although disappointed initially at being unable to share his success with Mary or his parents, it no longer mattered. It was strange.

Brian said he couldn't leave, but there was no need, where could he go, he was dead?

"Can you explain about Gwen yet, her role in this?"

"Unfortunately, no, not until I receive the confirmation. You've done remarkably well, Michael; I've never had the pleasure of witnessing a death like yours. I realise that sounds weird, but I'll explain that soon."

"You mean after you get your confirmation." Michael said with a hint of humorous sarcasm.

"Good to see you've retained your sense of humour, sometimes people lose it temporarily until they've made the adjustments," he said, smiling. "I died less than twenty years ago, and I'm still classed a learner at being a Seeker."

"So, now we just wait?"

"We just wait. Time has no relevance in the spiritual world."

"Speaking of time, why did I always return to the same day and time after a vision. Why the same woman revealing it? And the busker, what was his role?"

"It was the time of your death, Michael; you couldn't stay beyond that.

"The train departure time was nine-o'clock, surely I stayed beyond that?"

"What took hours in the living world was mere seconds in ours, Michael."

The woman was present to allow you to return to reality, a familiar face to calm the confusion. The busker's role was identical. Do you remember your great uncle Fred and great aunt Joyce, by any chance?"

"No, I have no memories, they died shortly after my birth."

"They did, but they played those roles to help you."

"They were my great Uncle and Aunt?"

"They were. Will I be able to meet them soon?"

"They're waiting for you as I speak."

The talking ceased, and they waited patiently in silence, though Brian kept smiling at Michael periodically.

"Sorry!" he said suddenly. "I didn't mean to make you feel uncomfortably, but you're my first and I'm expecting positive confirmation of my recommendation."

"Which you can't reveal yet!" Michael finished for him.

He looked at Michael, raising his eyebrows, smiled and fell quiet again.

Then the phone rang, making Michael jump.

Brian picked it up and responded to the caller.

"Yes! Yes, Wonderful, Fantastic! I'll tell him straight away. Thank you," he said, placing the phone down.

"I have the most wonderful news, but I want to shake your hand first. This is the most exciting day of my life; I mean my afterlife."

They shook hands, and he pumped Michael's as if there was no tomorrow, which Michael guessed there wasn't.

"Do you have your employment card still, Michael?"

Michael nodded, removed it from his shirt pocket, and handed it over. He opened it and lay it on the desk so Michael could see the stickers.

"On the side marked location, there are six boxes each containing a letter you earned: E, A, E, H, N and V. It would appear you've placed the letters in the wrong order, but that's not a problem. Stare at them and watch what happens."

Michael stared, not knowing what to expect. They lifted from the card, floated and reorganised themselves. Settling back on the card, he read the anagram of the letters. The word heaven stared back up at him.

"That shouldn't be a surprise to you, we've already established you are going there. Now look at the second block of letters under Job Title."

Again, Michael stared at the card and Brian read out the letters: N, A, L, E and G. They lifted from the card reorganising as the first group had, before settling. Michael stared at the word before look up at Brian in surprise.

"Congratulations Michael you're my first, the first Angel I've found to send upstairs."

His smile radiated around the room.

"What a Christmas Present this is, thank you Michael. It's rare outside of wartime to get anybody passing through here who died saving another's life. It happens, of course it does, but the cases are few. By doing that, it automatically makes you a candidate for the top job. But that alone is not enough; you must demonstrate the good of others comes first and naturally to you. Consideration of personal gain is an absolute no, and you passed every test we set. Gwen is an angel, sent to assist if the need was required. She was needed, and yet it was you the baby was named after. It's the affect you have on those you help.

"Wow, Muriel had an angel for a midwife. Cool!"

"Your mother and sister called you Angel for years, interpret that how you will. There are few jobs in the afterlife permitting contact with the living; your new job as an angel allows it, as does mine as a seeker. The job involves helping people around the world if the boss permits. He oversees every case. So, it's a natural perk of the job, you'll observe your family although never able to communicate with them, until they enter the afterlife. Any further questions, Michael, you need answering?" Brian finished. Although he suspected Michael had plenty, he wasn't surprised he couldn't think of one.

"Don't worry Michael, you'll receive full training for your duties, and many can answer questions you form later. When you pass through the door of my office, you'll enter the Kingdom of Heaven to begin your duties."

"I have a request, Brian. Will you walk through with me? Honestly, knowing what's ahead, and living up to the role and the expectations is daunting."

"Actually Michael, for you that's the easy part, just be yourself. I would be delighted to walk through with you. Remember, your physical life might be over, but your spiritual life is everlasting. There are people waiting for you Michael; Mary, your uncle and aunt... Shall we start your journey. It lies through there."

Standing, Brian opened the door and together they walked through into a veiled duvet of mist that immediately wrapped its embrace around them, gently caressing their bodies, before lifting and carrying them upwards.

"Ok Brian, this is kind of cool."

"It is, isn't it?"

C. S. Clifford has always been passionate about stories and storytelling. As a child he earned money singing at weddings in the church choir; the proceeds of which were spent in the local bookshop.

As a former primary teacher, he was inspired to start writing through the constant requests of the children he taught. He lives in Kent where, when not writing or promoting and teaching writing, he enjoys carpentry, sea and freshwater angling and exploring the history of his local countryside.